finding

hope

finding
hope

COLLEEN NELSON

DUNDURN
TORONTO

Copy editor: Natalie Meditsky
Design: Jennifer Gallinger
Cover design: Laura Boyle
Cover image: © Ungureanu Alexandra/123rf.com
Printer: Webcom

Library and Archives Canada Cataloguing in Publication

Nelson, Colleen author

    Finding Hope / Colleen Nelson.

Issued in print and electronic formats.

ISBN 978-1-4597-3245-2 (paperback).--ISBN 978-1-4597-3246-9 (pdf).--
ISBN 978-1-4597-3247-6 (epub)

    I. Title.

PS8627.E555F56 2016   jC813'.6   C2015-904577-0
                                          C2015-904578-9

2   3   4   5   20   19   18   17   16

 Conseil des Arts du Canada   Canada Council for the Arts   Canada   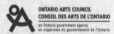 ONTARIO ARTS COUNCIL CONSEIL DES ARTS DE L'ONTARIO an Ontario government agency un organisme du gouvernement de l'Ontario

We acknowledge the support of the Canada Council for the Arts and the Ontario Arts Council for our publishing program. We also acknowledge the financial support of the Government of Canada through the Canada Book Fund and Livres Canada Books, and the Government of Ontario through the Ontario Book Publishing Tax Credit and the Ontario Media Development Corporation.

Care has been taken to trace the ownership of copyright material used in this book. The author and the publisher welcome any information enabling them to rectify any references or credits in subsequent editions.

— *J. Kirk Howard, President*

The publisher is not responsible for websites or their content unless they are owned by the publisher.

Printed and bound in Canada.

VISIT US AT
Dundurn.com | @dundurnpress | Facebook.com/dundurnpress | Pinterest.com/dundurnpress

Dundurn
3 Church Street, Suite 500
Toronto, Ontario, Canada
M5E 1M2

For Karen Deeley,
Nancy Chappell-Pollack,
and Gord Chappell

HOPE

Mom brandished an envelope above her head like a flag. "A letter just came for you."

I'd been waiting a month for that letter. Hopping off my bicycle, I let it tumble to the grass. Dry and scrubby, it crackled from lack of water. The summer had stretched endlessly and only now, with the hum of bugs in the air, did it show signs of coming to a close. "It's like someone didn't get the memo," Dad liked to say when the seasons didn't follow his timetable. Last two weeks of August should have meant deer flies and cooler nights, a hint of the chill that would be coming with autumn, but not this year.

I took the sealed envelope from her. "It's thick, that's a good sign," she said, her hands on my shoulders, not realizing how hard she was squeezing.

My hands shook. The tear I made was ragged and the letter got stuck. Finally, I pulled it free and unfolded it. "Ravenhurst School for Girls is pleased to inform you that you have been accepted for the coming school year." I didn't read past those words. Mom started screaming and hugging me.

I waited to feel something. A gush of relief or a flood of emotion, but there was nothing. Instead, I felt more rooted to the ragged wooden planks on the porch. A stubborn will to stay.

"Congratulations, Hope!" Mom said and pulled me into another hug. The letter was stuck between us, my arm at an awkward angle.

Ravenhurst had been Mom's idea. She'd done the research to find a school that took boarders in the city and then laid out her plan over dinner one night, peering at me with her fork hanging in mid-air. "Wouldn't you want to go there?" she'd asked. I looked at Dad, head down, shovelling mac and cheese into his mouth. "Get out of this place." She waved her fork around, as if "this place" meant nothing more than our house. Her eyes bugged out, begging me to agree with her.

"Uh-huh," I said. I didn't realize that my non-committal grunt would start a two-month long odyssey. Acceptance to a private school in the city meant letters from teachers, an exam, and then an interview. Mom had bought a navy, pleated skirt for me to wear and flat black shoes that pinched my toes. I'd hobbled through the atrium of the school, gazing up at a two-storey foyer encased in glass. Sunlight streamed in, reflecting off the marble floors. Our footsteps echoed, too small to fill the cavernous space.

I wasn't kidding myself, Mom wanted this more than I did. As usual, I'd gone along with her plans, not wanting to be the one who upset the delicate balance that existed in our family.

Our splintered family.

ERIC

Sometimes I watch them from the street. I tuck myself behind a tree or a parked car and watch them eat dinner. All three of them. Together. My chair: empty.

I keep waiting for a pull to go back, a desire to be part of that picture again. But it doesn't come. They are something else, separate from me. I can't remember a life where I was part of that. I know I was. Hope leaves photos for me sometimes in our stump. Some memories for me.

She doesn't know that the guy in the pictures—the hockey player, the kid smiling at the beach or raking leaves—is dead. She's pulling photos out of Mom's albums, quietly erasing me.

Tonight, I watch as Hope looks up from her plate and stares outside. Maybe she can sense me, her big brother, out here watching. Her eyes search, wanting something that isn't there. She turns to Mom, pulling her eyes away from me, reluctantly, I like to think.

She'll leave something for me later. Some treasure, in the stump.

I slink away, the heat suffocating, a hot, dry wind kicking up dust on the street. I'll find something to take away the dull ache watching my family gives me. A snort or a sniff or a prick to make it all go away.

HOPE

On the corner of our property, concealed in a thicket of prickly bushes, is a tree stump. Mythological in its presence, it's been there since we were kids. Like a portal to another world, it smells damp and earthy, the ground around it spongy and cool.

A dark hollow at its roots is our hiding spot. Today, Eric will find an apple, red and waxy; ten dollars of babysitting money, freshly earned, that never even made it into my wallet; and a shirt, one I found in his room.

I went in his bedroom last night, after dinner. Counting in my head to eighteen, I limit my snooping to as many seconds as his age. In eighteen seconds, I can rifle through one drawer or peruse one shelf of trophies, and then I force myself to leave. I need to make the secrets of his room last, like I'm slowly unwrapping a Christmas gift.

I left him a poem too, scratched onto grade eleven math notes, found under his bed. Eric used to call my poetry mental diarrhea, an excretion of words and phrases. He didn't understand my compulsion to solidify a thought. Like a conjurer, I swirled ideas into

something tangible—something that had meaning—
and put them on paper.

> Your chair
> Sits like
> A corpse
> At the table
> I moved it
> Away.

Making sure all the treasures were tucked into place,
I took a look around. Was he nearby? Sometimes I could
feel him, ghostlike beside me. But today there was nothing, no telltale signs he'd been there.

ERIC

I stared at the cigarette in my hand, thinking back to what I was like before the meth. Two years ago, I didn't even smoke. Now, I took whatever drugs I got offered. The smoke had burned down to the filter, but I kept sucking on it, inhaling the last wisps of a buzz held in the nicotine.

My real dad was a smoker. In the few pictures Mom kept of him, there was always a cigarette dangling from his fingers or one sitting in an ashtray beside him. Usually a beer too. He looked like a guy who liked to party.

Dick, Hope's dad, my step-father, didn't even drink. Maybe that was why Mom liked him; he was the opposite of my dad. A good role model for me, her young son.

But I turned out like this anyway.

A guy I knew drove up and rolled down the window. "Wanna ride?" He was off his night shift, kids were at school, wife at work. He was looking to buy and some company to get high with.

Dropping my cigarette on the road, I crushed it under my shoe and got into his minivan. "I'm tapped out, man. You mind spotting me a line?"

He pursed his lips and glowered at me. "I'm not a fucking ATM."

I shrugged. "You should've asked if I had cash *before* the invite." I grinned at him, leaning back against the seat.

"Fuck." He sighed and put the car into drive.

HOPE

At the spray pad, kids shrieked, wet hair matted against their heads. The air was heavy, with the promise of a storm on its way. No one would complain. We needed a good downpour, Mom and Dad agreed. The flowers had started to wither in the beds, the soil parched and cracking with fault lines.

I watched as two girls from my grade, Shauna and Leanne, giggled with some boys. Both of them had a roundness to their bodies, an extra layer that made them voluptuous. At fifteen, I was still as scrawny and prepubescent-looking as a twelve-year-old. With the attitude to match. Girls in Lumsville cared about parties, boys, who they could score pot off of. I was like a reverse magnetic attraction, repelling those "good times." I wanted no part of it.

Parents sat on the other side of the spray pad, watching their kids from picnic tables and throwing dirty looks at the squealing girls with their too-small bikini tops and jiggling flesh. The boys from school looked on appreciatively, jockeying for a better view, a closer angle. I had to look away. Even outside, I was on the outside.

The smell of pot wafted over. Like in any town where boredom was the number-one export, weed was easy to get here. I remembered the first time I saw Eric high. The telltale scent clung to him as he collapsed beside me on the couch, a goofy grin on his face. I didn't know what high looked like, but it was unsettling to my eleven-year-old self. He was talking and laughing like he was someone else.

That was how it began for Eric. From pot he graduated to meth, and anything else floating around Lumsville. A drug sucker-fish. An addict.

In moments of sobriety, he warned me not to start. He wanted better for me. I just wanted my brother back.

ERIC

Thunder rumbled. The storm hadn't hit yet, but there was static in the air. Like something heavy was about to be dropped. I needed a place to go, hide out till it passed.

Saturday night. Hope would be babysitting for the Kellers. Not like her friends, Shauna and Leanne, who I saw at parties sometimes, or in the park. They ignored me, turning their lips up in a sneer, like I was dirty. Like they were fucking *embarrassed* by me. I'd known them since they were five and now they acted like they were better than me.

The back door at the Kellers' house was locked. I gave it a jiggle. The glass in the window rattled. Air conditioning. All the windows were shut. How good would a cool blast of bottled air feel? God, to be cool for ten minutes. I hopped on the spot. My body felt electric, a current running through me, shooting out of my toes. Meth made every nerve come alive. I wanted to dance, run, twist, and jump; all the energy hidden when I was sober crackled when the drug was in me.

I knocked. "Hope!" I yelled. The kitchen lights were

off. I waited, bouncing. Knocked again, pressed my nose up to the glass, peering in. My face squished against the glass, breath hot and foggy. And there she was, standing in the doorway.

My little sister. Small. She still looked like a kid: gangly arms, long, brown hair, too-white skin, and knobby knees like a stork. A thump in my chest when I saw her.

She took a breath, her mouth hardened with determination. In three steps, she was across the kitchen, the lock clicking open.

"Hey," I said, low but jittery. The electricity was still firing through me, like a pinball let loose.

"You can't come in," she said.

"Nah, I know. Can I crash somewhere? It's gonna piss down soon."

"Wait here." She disappeared, small feet beating a trail somewhere I couldn't follow. And then back. The sky flashed with sheet lightning. A moth beat its wings against the porch light. "You can sleep in the garage at home. I'll bring you food in the morning." She passed me the key for the garage, spinning it off her keyring. A blast of AC hit me, I breathed it in. The hot and cold clashed. Electricity zipped over my skin. "Did you eat?" she asked.

I grinned at her. My teeth felt huge, gargantuan in my mouth, like a horse's.

She left the door open, and I stuck my head in, rolling it around in the cool air, feeling it shrink, like my dick in cold lake water.

A few slices of pizza, limp, heavy with shiny cheese and pepperoni, on a paper towel. "From Luigi's?" I asked. We used to order from there all the time, or the whole team would go after a game.

Before. So much life had happened before.

She nodded, and I couldn't remember what she was nodding about. I just took the pizza, pocketed the key in my pants, and tripped off the back steps.

HOPE

I heard Dad's car roll up and looked at Mom, wide-eyed. He was supposed to work late on Wednesdays. What was he doing home so early?

Mom moved her mouth soundlessly, like a fish. Eric was at the kitchen table, eating a sandwich, drinking a glass of Pepsi, bubbles percolating up past the ice cubes. He was in no rush.

She went to the kitchen window, looked out. Dad would be in the garage, puttering, making his way into the house. She bit her lip, chewing off dead skin. "I could pack that up for you," she offered, stressed now.

Not much riled Dad. He was mellow, liked to sit in front of the TV and watch real-life cop dramas. But he'd had it with Eric. And Mom had promised she wouldn't let him come over anymore. "Tough love, Ev," Dad had said gently, urging her to agree. "It's for his own good. The only way he'll hit rock bottom is if we let him." That was months ago, before we knew what kind of a monster Eric's addiction would turn into.

"It's my house too," Eric mumbled.

"No, it's not." Firm Mom. It took all her strength to say it. "Not while you're using."

Eric stood up fast, the chair bucking away from him. His eyes flashed.

"Shush!" she calmed him, trying to placate, keep the peace. "Don't."

In my head, words formed a poem, aligning themselves.

Do not.

Use.

Yell.

Come back.

Leave.

Dad was walking up the path to the house. It was his sore neck that had brought him home early: occupational hazard for a mechanic. He was rubbing it, squeezing the muscly, hard flesh. Mom would be coaxed into rubbing it for him while he watched TV later. He'd moan with relief as her hands kneaded it like dough.

"Hiya, Dick," Eric said before Dad was even all the way in the kitchen. I winced. Used to be *Dad*, sometimes *Richard*. Now it was *Dick*.

Dad looked at Mom, eyes narrowing, nostrils flaring. He ignored Eric. We stood like a stage play, each of us hitting our mark. I stayed mute, escaping in my head with a poem.

> The daffodil curtains
> Flutter in your wake
> Sunlight beams penetrate
> Fading fabric

> Glowing with creature comfort
> To announce your arrival.

I wished I had a pen and paper so I could capture the words before they flitted away like smoke.

They all started talking at the same time. Mom, apologizing to one but meaning it to the other, Dad railing against her enabling Eric. Eric, mad as hell at everyone.

But not me. Please, not me. I backed out of the room. No one would notice.

Their raised voices reached a crescendo. One door slammed, then another. There were angry, tearful words from Mom and more yelling.

Digging in my desk, I found a pen and jotted down the words, letting my mind roll over them, like they were a delicious bite I didn't want to let go of. I created that. Before, there was nothing, shapeless ideas floating in the air. I brought them together. I had power over the words, they bent to my will.

They would end up on my wall. Tacked, layered over another one.

A patchwork of poetry in my now-quiet house.

ERIC

Where did it begin? In lucid moments, when I wasn't jangling for want of a fix, or high, I'd remember, trace it back like a tangled ball of yarn.

The pot was for fun. Me and the guys, hanging out. Then Matt's older brother brought some other shit, stuff for us to try in the basement.

God, the first time that shit went into my body, I felt like I was flying. Nothing could touch me. Everything in my life made sense, was exactly the way it was supposed to be.

All the heat and anger that boiled in me when I was sober, disappeared on meth.

Hockey was gone, done. It didn't matter what I put in my body. It was an empty vessel, something to be used. And it felt so fucking good.

When I catch my reflection in a window or a washroom mirror, it takes me a second to process who it is staring back. My own face freaks the shit out of me.

Hair: unwashed, flat with grease. Scabs on my face, smudges of black under haunted eyes. Gaunt, skeletal, ears and teeth that stick out because the rest of my face isn't big enough to support them anymore.

Something crinkled in my pocket. I hoped for money, a forgotten five-dollar bill, but it wasn't, it was one of Hope's poems.

Remember the swings
Flying up
Never landing
Stomach floating and dropping
You'd push me
Higher.
I never wanted you to stop.
Now I say
Stop.

Sometimes when I read them, they made me cry. Because she still knew me. She hadn't given up.

I plod. Walking from one park bench to another, hiding out by the tracks, in a thicket of trees. I had my spots. Most of the day, I slept anywhere. I got kicked out of places where they used to know my name. Used to fucking bang on the glass at a game, shouting my name! *"Give 'em hell, Eric!"* Roaring when I scored, top shelf in overtime on a breakaway. Teammates clobbering me with jubilation. Everyone knew my name then.

Today, I was hanging out by the grocery store, sitting on the sidewalk. A song ran through my head. "Good Old Hockey Game." I muttered the few words I remembered. This was how I spent my days. Sleep, plod, sit. Get high. They stretched one into the other.

Didn't know what day of the week it was most of the time.

Someone stuck a fiver in my face. I didn't look up, but saw her old-lady shoes beside me on the sidewalk. The beige kind, with thick rubber soles. "There's a lunch special on at the diner today. Tell them Gertie sent you."

"Thanks," I mumbled, crumpling it in my hand.

I couldn't look up. Didn't want to see her face, the pity or disgust on it. I didn't even want her money, given with a condition: food, not drugs.

The lyrics to the song came all of a sudden, like a thunderclap in my head. *Now the final flick, of a hockey stick, and one gigantic scream: "The puck is in! The home team wins!" At the good old hockey game.* I started laughing, cackled like a crow, I was so happy I'd figured it out. From the corner of my eye, I saw the old-lady shoes take off.

Five bucks was enough to score me a high.

I started walking to Tyler's place, an old shed outside of town. The dusty road stretched out till forever in front of me. If Tyler was cooking, he'd let me crash there and keep him company. Maybe spot me a sample too. Reason enough to keep plodding.

HOPE

I knew he'd come by today. I'd left a note at the stump telling him Mom and Dad were going into town for a movie. He'd have the run of the kitchen and a shower if he wanted it.

Eric came in through the back door, which I left unlocked, despite Dad's rule. "Hey," he said, coming up to the couch, a banana in his hand, already unpeeled and half-eaten. He wasn't high. His eyes didn't jerk around like they were on a marionette string. "What's up?" His voice flat.

I moved over on the couch so he'd sit beside me. Pictures of us as kids lined the mantel. First day of school; Eric in his hockey gear, a menacing grin on his face and another photo of him holding a trophy. Like a time capsule, we didn't change in those photos.

"Remember I told you about that school, Ravenhurst?" He gave a noncommittal nod. "I got accepted." I waited for a reaction, not sure what it would be. His rages were unpredictable.

He raised his eyebrows. "You're leaving." Not a question.

I nodded. "Next Monday. School starts Tuesday." Things he'd know if he still went to school.

He tossed his banana peel onto the coffee table. It sat there, limp and empty. "So, that's it, huh? Mom got one of us out of this fucking shithole." *Not the one she'd expected, either.* He didn't say it out loud, but we both knew it was true. Stuck here her whole life, Mom's biggest regret was staying in Lumsville. She should have left when she graduated, but she'd already met Eric's dad. Five years later and she was the widowed mom of a three-year-old and needed her parents nearby. Then she met Dad and had me.

> Trapped.
> Every fingernail scrapes
> On shut doors,
> Ripping off.
> At least the blood
> can escape.

She wasn't going to let Eric and me fall into the same trap. Her plans for us had always included leaving Lumsville. I would go to a big city for university, that was a given. Money from my grandparents was banked for tuition. But Eric, his ticket out had been hockey.

He'd been scouted the year he turned fifteen. Coaches wanted him on their teams, they took him to special practices and tournaments in places so far he had to fly there. Dad worked overtime to pay for it. Mom would flutter with excitement when coaches called to talk with her about Eric's future. She'd tousle his hair with pride when he walked in the door.

And then it all changed. One day, his coach dropped him off after a tournament in a town too far for us to go. Mom asked Eric how it went, but he ignored her, went to his room, and shut the door. He didn't come down till the next day, for school. Mom blamed his moodiness on hormones, his real father, the pressure of hockey.

Finally, I think she blamed herself. She'd pushed him too hard. He burnt himself out. Somewhere along the way, he found meth. Or meth found him.

It was a win for me by default, because all the money that used to be funnelled into Eric's hockey would pay for me to attend the Ravenhurst School for Girls.

"You could come visit me," I said, knowing it was a stupid thing to say. How would he get there? Drive to the city with Mom?

He nodded like it was a possibility. Sometimes we kept the lie going, pretending things were normal.

I tucked my hands between my knees and looked at him, my mouth twitching with an unasked question.

"What?" he asked.

"If I'm not around, how are you going to, you know, manage?" *Without me?* No one would be around to drop food off for him, or clothes. Or money. I know Mom gave him some when she could, but it came at a price. He had to be clean and sneak around so Dad didn't see him. "Are you going to be okay?"

"Pfft." He blew air out of his cheeks like it was no big deal. "Yeah."

"Really? Because I've left you a lot of money this summer. What are you going to do without it?" Twenty percent of my babysitting earnings went to the stump and he was acting like it didn't matter.

His eyes got cold. "I don't have a bed, or food, either, but I'm surviving."

A dig. A reminder that I was still at home and he wasn't. I bit back my retort. I'd stuck out my neck for him a hundred times.

His words hurt. I felt my insides curdle. It was his choice to live this way, I reminded myself. We'd all given him chances, even Dad. But when he'd stolen Mom's bank card and drained her account of hundreds of dollars, that was the last straw. Mom and Dad had the locks changed, and left a pile of his clothes on the front steps.

"You could stop using," I said, "and move back."

The suggestion hung between us. He pinched his mouth closed and shut down. I'd wrecked his coming over. Now he'd leave angry, slamming the door and disappearing for days.

It wasn't my fault he was a user.

But somehow, I felt like I'd let *him* down.

ERIC

I'd acted like it didn't matter. Like losing Hope was no big deal.

But inside, I shrivelled.

And then felt like an asshole, because the real reason I didn't want her to go was because it meant I'd have to find money somewhere else.

I told her it was for food. She believed me because she wanted to.

I wished it were the truth. I fooled myself into believing that I went to see her because I missed her, but the reality was I needed my next high and Hope would give me the money to make it happen.

I didn't blame her for leaving, though. She was smart to get out of this shithole. I should have gone when I had the chance, now it was too late. Hockey, my ticket out of Lumsville, was done. I'd sold my equipment months ago, using meth to burn away the hurt.

I couldn't think about hockey anymore without thinking about *him*. The two were intertwined. I swear, I could even smell *him* on my gear. He'd infested it.

I wanted to kill the germs he'd planted in me, but I

didn't know how. They grew like dark, twisting vines, coiling through my insides. Suffocating me from the inside out.

"Fuck," I mumbled. The meth was messing with my mind. I was starting to think like a fucking poet too. Spewing mental diarrhea, just like my sister.

HOPE

Mom and I in the car, contained. Pale wheat fields stretched out to the horizon on each side of the road. The sky was a watery blue but grew darker as it met the land. Occasionally, a farmhouse or service road dotted the landscape.

> Harvest
> Farmers (wheat killers).
> Threshers; the monsters that mow it
> down
> A battle
> Against what they sowed.
> Irony of the prairies.

Grabbing an old gas receipt, I jotted the words down and stuffed it into my pocket.

"Oh," Mom sighed, "I forgot to pack your bathing suit."

Like I was going to the moon. Ravenhurst was three hours away, door to door. She'd be seeing me in less than three weeks when she came in for my birthday. So far, no swimming parties were planned.

But still, her constant second-guessing made me nervous, like I wasn't prepared. She was quiet, comparing the list of things she'd wanted to pack for me to what had actually made it into my bag. The last time we'd barrelled down the highway had been for the interview. She'd been more nervous then, gripping the steering wheel. Dad had come too, even though he hated driving. Hated leaving Lumsville. But he was willing to do it for me.

"If you get in or don't get in, it doesn't matter to me, Hope. I'm proud of you, no matter what." He'd craned his neck back from the front seat and given me an encouraging smile. He'd shaved that morning, but already stubbly whiskers had appeared on his chin. If it had been up to him, I'd have stayed in Lumsville. But Mom was determined that going away to school was the right choice.

How many times had Dad said the same words to Eric? When he left for a tournament: "Win or not, I'm proud of you." Or a tryout: "Make the team or not, I'm proud of you." He'd been Eric's dad since Eric was four years old, marrying Mom because he loved her and couldn't stand the thought of a boy not having a dad, that's what Mom told me once. "He's a good man. I'm lucky to have him."

Not anymore, according to Eric.

Our family used to be normal. We did things other families did together: barbecues in the backyard, rounds of minigolf, car trips, and movie nights. Those days ended when Eric started using. Now, every event screamed with his absence. We filled our lives with distractions. Like getting me into this school.

Mom had surprised me at the interview, pulling out a sheaf of papers, scraps, napkins, old history tests, whatever had been closest for me to write on. "I brought these for you," she told the interviewers. "She's so talented, I wanted you to see."

My poems. Not meant for public consumption. I'd blushed, watching the interview panel read my thoughts. And after, when we were driving home, words strung themselves together in my head like a gemstone necklace. A poem about the interview. I wrote it on my palm with my fingertip, trying to imprint onto my body. It had ended up on my wall that night.

> Poems plucked
> Like wildflowers from my wall.
> A bouquet of fragrant words
> My gift to you
> Taken.

I was leaving everything behind: my home, my parents, my school, and Eric. I stared morosely out the window. The city skyline stretched across the horizon, hazy with heat. Swaths of farmland would give way to urban sprawl soon, pulling me farther and farther away from who I was.

ERIC

Through the space between the fence boards, I could see Dick flipping burgers. One hand at his waist, the other holding a spatula. Mom and Hope sat on lawn chairs, sipping tall glasses of iced tea.

Hope had left a note for me in the stump, inviting me to her going-away party. Eternal optimist. As if it was something to celebrate.

Through the sliver of space I saw a metallic cellophane BON VOYAGE banner taped across the deck railing. And there were balloons.

This was what my life should have been. A going-away party on the deck, the hockey team over to celebrate. Instead, I was out here, on the other side, fighting my way through waist-high thistles and prickly dandelion weeds.

I hoped this was what Hope wanted, and that Mom hadn't bullied her into it. It had always been Mom's dream for us to get out of Lumsville. Hockey, school—whatever would take us far away from this town.

I pulled myself away from the fence, kicking at a rock in the alley. A weird pain ached in my gut. I tried to shrug it off as hunger, but I knew that wasn't what it was. I was going to miss my sister.

I'd score tonight. She'd left me some money with the note. Maybe she knew I'd want to celebrate on my own.

HOPE

"Call if you need *anything*," Mom said. She brushed out a non-existent wrinkle on my quilt, a hand-me-down with worn edges that smelled like home. "Well, I guess … " she trailed off. It was time for her to go.

It had been my choice to come here, I reminded myself. Mom had planted the idea, but I'd been the one to do all the work, insisting during the interview that it had always been my dream to attend Ravenhurst. And when we'd driven through the gates and up the circular driveway, I'd gazed up at the imposing brick building and gotten butterflies.

But now that I was sitting on a mattress that felt thin and hard, and nothing looked familiar, I got a lump in my throat. Once she left, I was on my own.

I rubbed the thin fabric of the quilt between my fingers and avoided looking at Mom. I could hear the tears in her voice.

"I guess you'll go down for dinner soon," she said. "Meet some of the other students. They'll all be arriving today."

I nodded. My roommate had already set up her side of the room. Posters, a colourful comforter, and stuffed animals made her space look lived in.

Mom stood up. "I better get going." She rubbed my shoulder and I thought about asking her to take me back to Lumsville with her. I didn't want to go to Ravenhurst after all. But spending another year at Lumsville High School wasn't the right fit either.

"Here." She pulled a ribbon-bound journal out of her purse and thrust it at me. An orange leather cover embossed with daisies, heavy with unused pages. "It's a journal, for your poems."

I tried to say thank you, but the words got stuck in my throat, tears sprang to my eyes. "Thanks," I croaked, clutching it against my chest. I'd used scribblers and scrap paper, but I'd never had a dedicated journal before.

"I thought it might help. In case you get homesick. You've always been good at writing down how you feel, even if you don't say anything."

> Shreds of emotion
> Laid bare on my wall,
> Like mental graffiti.

I wrapped my arms around her neck, wishing I didn't have to let go.

ERIC

We used to play against Wolf Creek in an exhibition game once a year. Start of season, we'd go to the reserve on a rented bus, our families following behind in their cars. The rez kids were scrappy and fast.

My guys, the Lumsville Hornets, were always keyed up for the Wolf Creek game. It set the tone for the rest of the season. The crowd was hyped-up too, our parents' voices echoing off the ice, the noise from air horns and cow bells blending into one deafening roar.

The Wolves banged their sticks on the boards before they hit the ice. It intimidated the shit out of me the first time I heard it. But then I scored on my first shift. I looked up by chance and saw Mom standing and clapping for me, hugging Hope. My team skated over to slap my helmet, but nothing felt as good as seeing Mom bursting with pride in the bleachers.

The last time we played in Wolf Creek, I scored the game winner, in overtime. Instead of looking at Mom, I'd turned to the bench. Coach Williams gave a fist punch in the air and slapped his clipboard. Then he pointed at me. A silent, triumphant signal, like, "I knew you could do it." The team unloaded off the bench and clobbered me, overjoyed at the win. When we got to the dressing room, Coach took a minute to single me out. Making sure I knew how much the team relied on me. What a special player I was.

HOPE

The rough wool skirt scratched against my legs. I yanked my navy socks up so they skimmed my knees and took a deep breath. The Ravenhurst uniform required a navy V-neck sweater and black shoes. I'd been living in tank tops and denim cut-offs all summer. The heavy fabric felt alien against my skin.

I pulled my hair up into a ponytail and surveyed the final result. My eyes, the same icy blue as Mom's, stared back at me. I was almost pretty, but nothing matched up. Eyes that were too big, a nose that had a bump in the middle, and lips that sat small and puckered, too far from my chin. I was awkward-looking.

Not like Eric. He was good-looking, or had been. With light green eyes and a confident strut, he used to walk around town like he owned it. His hair was blond, like his dad's. He'd let it grow when he played hockey, so it stuck out of his hockey helmet and flew behind him when he skated. Now it hung limp and unwashed.

In Lumsville, I was the outsider, the one who didn't know the right thing to say or wear, who laughed at jokes too late and then stopped laughing altogether. What was the point? Every year, I hoped that a new family would move into town. With a daughter my age. We'd have an instantaneous connection and become inseparable.

That never happened. But Ravenhurst had. Maybe my mythical friend was waiting for me in the dorms.

"Please let them like me," I whispered, squeezing my hands into fists in a silent prayer.

The door opened and Cassie, my roommate, tore into the room. She was fresh from the shower and her robe hung off one shoulder. "Shit!" she wailed, frantic. "I'm late!"

We'd barely said hello yesterday. She'd tiptoed in just before "lights out" and had whispered a greeting in the dark. Her parents had taken her out for dinner. From a small town five hours east of the city, she spoke quickly and laughed loudly.

"Can you pass me those socks?" she asked from her bed, where she sat rubbing lotion onto her legs. "Thanks!" she said with a relieved grin and yanked them on. They stuck to her legs like sausage casings. I caught a flash of dimpled, cherub thighs as she wriggled into them.

"Oh," she cried, pulling back her blanket. "Seen my sweater?"

Even though I wanted to get to the dining hall and find a place to sit before it got crowded, I helped her search. "Is this it?" I asked, pulling a sleeve out from under a pile of books on her desk chair. The rest of the sweater followed.

"Thanks!" she said and took it from me. Her hair had left splotches of wetness on her robe. "So, where are you from?"

"Lumsville. It's small, you probably don't know it. Three hours west of the city."

"You've probably never heard of Waterton, either. Dad got posted there for work and it's in the boondocks, hours from anywhere. Small towns." She shrugged, as if they were a lost cause. "What's Lumsville like?"

I gave her a wry smile. "About the same as Waterton, probably."

"I started at Ravenhurst last year," she said, vigorously towel drying her hair. "My brother's at Melton Prep. That's, like, the boys' school to RH. We do activities with them sometimes. Do you have any brothers or sisters?"

She turned around, her naked back to me, and slipped on her bra, hooking it closed in one quick motion and turned back to me. I looked away, shy for her. "Just a brother. He's older and done school." Sort of. I didn't explain that school was more done with him than he with it. I gave a silent sigh of regret for him. Even here, at boarding school, his choices loomed over me.

Cassie started to button her shirt. "Maybe it'll be different for you, but these girls are a prickly bunch." I didn't have time to ask what she meant because she glanced at a clock on her nightstand and groaned. "Ugh! Is that the time? I'm gonna be late my first day. Do you mind grabbing me some breakfast? Toast or something? I'll meet you in the cafeteria after I dry my hair." Cassie was already turning on her dryer and didn't look at me when I gave a reluctant wave and left.

The dining area wasn't fancy, but with long tables and benches, it could hold all the boarders, plus the day students. The smell of toast and sizzling bacon wafted out from an industrial-style kitchen. I followed the other girls as they took trays from the rolling rack at the entrance and stood in line for food. Staff bustled behind the counter, refilling vats of scrambled eggs and sausages.

Too nervous to eat, I didn't pause at the French toast or hash browns, even though they smelled delicious. A few pieces of toast for Cassie and a lonely bowl of cereal were all that I carried to a table as far in the back as I could get.

I watched the other girls. Most of them had tweaked their uniform in some way, by un-tucking their blouse so the shirttails hung out or by flipping up the collar. A few of them had slouchy socks that hung over their shoes, not the knee-highs that I wore, which looked juvenile, like I should be playing on the monkey bars at recess.

Three girls walked in and others shuffled aside to make room for them in line. They'd all rolled up the waistband of their skirts so the hem grazed mid-thigh. I felt like a country church mouse watching them. Their laughter was high-pitched and cackling, hard to miss first thing in the morning.

Scanning the line, I waited for Cassie. Her toast was growing cold. A sudden stab of longing for the breakfast table at home made my cereal turn into tasteless mush.

The girls with the short skirts scanned the dining hall for a table. One of them, tall with long, dark hair and a gash of red lipstick, spotted mine, empty except for me. She nudged the other two and nodded in my direction. I hurriedly tossed the half-finished bowl of cereal back onto the tray and wrapped up Cassie's toast in a napkin. I didn't want company.

But I was too slow. They were at my table, standing over me. All three had long hair. Besides the tall girl, the other two were in varying stages of blondness. One had a big nose, big eyes, and pouty lips. Unusual-looking but striking.

The other was the shortest of the three. Her hair, betraying its true origins, was fluffy; curls at her temples had rebelled against the straightening iron. Well-tanned and cute in a stereotypical cheerleader sort of way.

The first girl, with the scarlet lips, appraised me. "Are you leaving?"

I nodded, sliding my tray to the edge of the table. The other two backed up slightly to make room for me, but she didn't. I had to swing my legs wide to avoid her as I got off the bench.

"You're new." It was a statement, with an undertone of disapproval.

I met her eyes. Green, wide-set over high cheekbones and a square jaw. She was pretty, but there was no softness to her.

Again, I nodded. I could feel her eyes on me as I picked up my tray and moved off the bench. I looked up quickly, once, as I was leaving. The girl looked through me, as if I wasn't there.

Cassie waved at me from the entrance, her blond hair bouncing behind her as she walked across the room. Glancing behind me, she made a face. "Did they kick you out?"

"No, I was done, sort of." I passed her the napkin-wrapped toast and put my soupy cereal leftovers on the refuse cart.

"Did Lizzie talk to you?" Cassie asked.

"The one with the brown hair? Not really." Cassie grabbed a packet of jam and a knife and found an empty stool along a counter near the exit. She sat down and smeared jam on her toast, and took some loud, crunchy bites.

"She can be a real bitch, so watch out. Do *not* get on her bad side." Red jam glued crumbs to her top lip.

I snorted. "I kinda got that. What's her deal?"

Cassie licked the crumbs off the corner of her mouth and shrugged. "Everyone listens to Lizzie. By tomorrow, all the girls' skirts will be like hers." She stood up. It was almost time to get to first period. "Her friends are Emily, the short one, and Vivian, who's actually really smart and nice, but Lizzie sucked her in last year. We used to be friends." I noticed the emphasis on *used to*. "There's my field hockey friends." She waved to a group heading toward us. I pasted a smile on my face, but Cassie brushed past me with no introductions. She and her girlfriends barrelled out the doors.

I was left standing alone, again, with a ridiculous smile plastered on my face.

ERIC

The Wolf Creek kids came into town sometimes, sitting on the edge of a pickup that rumbled down Main Street. The kids all knew me, or knew of me. Some of them played for the Wolves and had something to prove. Taking out the star player for the Hornets was bragging rights, even if I didn't play anymore.

Even if I was sleeping all afternoon on a park bench.

Hope didn't ask about the bloodstains anymore. Or the broken face. She didn't want to know and I didn't want to tell her.

If I'd been in the city, I could have found a place to stay, but out here, no one wanted to admit kids like me existed. The meth got cooked, sold out of the back door of someone's shed in the middle of nowhere. And kids eager to fight the boredom of small-town living bought it. I'd become a walking cliché. Pathetic.

Only, it wasn't boredom that had led me to this.

Sometimes I thought about my dad, what I would have been like if he'd been around more, or for longer. I guess you can't miss what you never had, but still, I miss him. The idea of him. I talk to him a lot, especially when I'm high, wanting him here and blaming him 'cause he isn't.

Mom wanted Dick to be that guy. Sold us to him as a package deal. But it never took. The same way he'd never love me as his own, I could never let him take the place of the guy I wished had never left.

My real dad was a long-haul truck driver. He'd go all the way up to Alaska or down to Texas. Gone for most of my first years, he was just a shadowy figure, like a cardboard cut-out in my mind, taking up space but without any substance, one-dimensional.

Sometimes, I pictured my dad on the bench beside me and talked to him. I probably looked crazy, but I didn't care. The conversation would be going great until I looked over and saw Coach Williams instead of Dad. Coach would be wearing his AAA ALL-STARS warm-up jacket and smiling at me. He'd lay a hand on my shoulder and give it a squeeze like he used to before I'd go out for a shift. A signal that everything was going to be okay.

Thanks, Coach, I thought and shook my head. A small part of me still missed him.

And I hated that part.

HOPE

I couldn't sleep. A branch outside scratched against the window in front of my desk. During the day, a blackbird had perched on it, surveying the field below, its caws a warning and a greeting. Cassie's gentle snores rumbled through the room, and no matter which way I turned, no position felt comfortable. Light from the moon shone into our room, creating shadows where there shouldn't have been any.

Tossing off my quilt, I tiptoed to the door, grabbed my key, and slid out into the hallway. To see a place empty that was usually so busy felt eerie. Sconces on the wall emitted a low hum and illuminated the hall with an orangey glow. Being out of my room after hours was against the rules. Just a quick trip to the washroom, and then straight back to bed.

I heard voices as soon as I pushed open the heavy door. It was too late to back out. There was a flurry of commotion, a stall door banged shut, a faucet started to gush. Then a sigh of relief when they saw it was another student and not Ms. Harrison, the dorm monitor.

"You scared the shit out of us!" Lizzie groaned, drying her hands. The two blonds from the cafeteria, Emily and Vivian, were with her. They looked at me suspiciously as I took a few more steps into the washroom. Tiled floor to ceiling, with a bank of sinks and mirrors on one wall and toilet and shower stalls on the other, the girls sat on a bench that stretched through the middle of the room.

"I have to pee," I told them, realizing how ridiculous I sounded. What other reason would I be in the washroom at midnight?

Lizzie snorted. "Go for it."

Fighting back a blush of embarrassment, I walked past them into the farthest cubicle. Their whispers echoed in the room, punctuating the silence. It was awkward, three people on the others side of the door listening to me pee. My stubborn bladder refused to let anything go. Performance anxiety. But now that I was in the washroom, I couldn't leave without going.

Closing my eyes, I tried to pretend they weren't a few metres away and forced my bladder to relax.

On the other side of the stall door, there was a commotion. "Emily, watch the bottle!" But too late, there was a crash and the sound of shattering glass. A few shards skittered across the floor and landed at my feet.

"Shit! You are such a fucking klutz!" Lizzie's voice, hissing.

"Come on, before Ms. Harrison gets in here!"

A rush of footsteps, the door opened and closed, and then silence. I was left alone in the washroom, with a broken bottle of booze slowly leaking toward me.

ERIC

I pulled a gift from Hope out of the hollow space in the stump, then tore through the bubble wrap and red bag to get at what lay inside.

A bomber jacket, distressed black leather and quilted lining. I held it up to my nose, breathing in the pungent animal-skin odour. The jacket was heavy, the leather soft and thick despite its weathered look. It must have cost her a lot of babysitting money.

My heart lurched at the thought of my sister. Ordering it online and leaving it here for me to find, days after she'd gone. I'd come here on a whim, knowing she was in the city at her new school. I'd been hoping for some money, I won't lie, but also one of her crazy poems, or a picture she'd pilfered from Mom's photo albums. Anything to show she hadn't forgotten me.

And it was this. A jacket that must have cost her a couple hundred dollars.

I rubbed a cuff, ribbed like a sweater, and ran the zipper up and down, hooking and unhooking the teeth.

I slipped my arms into the sleeves. Heavy on my shoulders and stiff, it weighed me down, grounding me.

I pulled my collection of photos and poems out of the pocket of my cargo shorts and stuffed them into a pocket of the jacket. It was too hot to wear a jacket like this, but I didn't care. I wanted it to mould to my body, become part of me, like armour.

I kicked the bag back under the stump. It rustled against the carpet of dead leaves and twigs, garish even in the filtered light of the thicket.

She'd bought it to keep me warm this winter, hedging a bet that I wasn't coming home.

You think you know me so fucking well? I thought. A hard lump of anger rose in my throat, because she probably did.

HOPE

I felt Lizzie's eyes on me as soon as I walked into the common room. With brown leather couches and beige walls, it looked utilitarian and homey at the same time. A gas fireplace in the middle of the room with a TV mounted above it was the focal point, but groupings of chairs all over the room meant girls were able to find private space if they wanted it.

I'd intended to beeline for the dormitory hallway and bypass the common room altogether. Ms. Harrison had given me a stern lecture last night. She'd caught me leaving the washroom and demanded to know who else had been in there. I'd lied, insisting I'd just walked in, saw the broken bottle, and was going to tell her. She'd clutched her bathrobe around her and pushed her wire-framed glasses farther up her nose. *Honest*, I'd told her. *Smell my breath*.

That morning, we'd all woken up to an email informing us that anyone caught drinking on school property would be suspended indefinitely.

"It's Hope, right?" Vivian appeared in front of me.

I nodded, shifting my books.

"Come sit with us." She tilted her head toward the couch in the centre of the room. Lizzie and Emily were there, books spread out around them, but their attention was more focused on phones than on studying.

I hesitated as Vivian walked across the room. Lizzie looked at me with a "What are you waiting for?" expression.

Perching on an armchair beside the couch, I waited for one of them to say something. No one did. Instead, six thumbs pecked at phones, sending texts. I stood up to leave. "Where are you going?" Lizzie asked. Her bright red lipstick intense, memorable against her pale skin.

"I have to study," I said, annoyed. She cast a glance at Emily and Vivian, both looking up from their phones.

"Study with us."

All three stared at me. "We owe you for last night," Emily said with a meaningful look at the other two. "What did you tell her?" *Her* meaning Ms. Harrison, the prim dorm monitor who had chosen to spend her life supervising boarding students.

I sat back down and leaned toward them. "That I'd just gotten there and found the mess. And that I hadn't seen anyone."

Emily gave a relieved laugh. "See? I told you she wouldn't blab."

Lizzie didn't look convinced. "Did you read the email she sent this morning? We'd get kicked out if someone told on us." Her words were a threat.

"I'm not going to tell on you," I said, irritated at her implication. Of all the people at this school, I wondered if anyone else was as well-versed in secret keeping as me.

Vivian leaned forward, her blue eyes bulging slightly. "We're meeting tomorrow night in their room." She nodded at Lizzie and Emily. "You should come too. At midnight."

"Maybe," I said, knowing that a nighttime drinking session wasn't worth the chance of getting caught by Ms. Harrison.

Lizzie gave a snort of laughter. "And *I* told *you*"—she looked pointedly at Emily—"that she's not Raven material. Never mind," she said to me so condescendingly my skin crawled, "you're probably so clean you squeak."

The disdain in her eyes reminded me of every girl in Lumsville who'd shunned me, deciding I wasn't cool enough or daring enough to hang out with her.

I had a chance right now to be part of something, more than just the kid sister to a hockey star. I could reinvent myself. And maybe, at Ravenhurst, that meant rolling up my skirt and sneaking through the hallways in the middle of the night.

I tossed Lizzie an offhand smile, as if her comment hadn't bothered me. "Tomorrow at midnight. Should I bring anything?"

Vivian gave Lizzie a victorious smirk and smiled at me. "Just yourself."

I settled back into the chair and took out my phone. I didn't have anyone to text but pretended I did, thumbing a fake message to myself.

ERIC

My dad's grave is in a cemetery outside of town. No stand-up gravestone, just a small marker flush with the grass, beside his parents'. In a far corner, off the walking path, it's hard to find unless you're looking for it. Perfect place to smoke a joint or have a long chat.

Mom never took me here when I was a kid. She didn't live in the past, said it was like dredging up the bottom of a riverbed, just a bunch of gunk she'd get stuck in. And, if I asked about my dad, she'd tell me I had one, Richard, and wasn't I lucky.

I used to think I was lucky. Blessed with a wicked slapshot and a skating stride that scouts drooled over. Parents who wrote cheques so I could fly all over the country and play with the best teams. I even got to go to a tournament in the Czech Republic when I was fifteen.

But shit happens and it turned out I wasn't so lucky.

Richard turned into Dick. I got locked out of the house because addicts weren't welcome. As if tough love could fix things.

I started thinking about my dad more, wondering what my life would have been like if he'd still been around. I trolled through the cemetery looking at grave-stones until I found the one with his name on it.

Crouching down over the marker, I wondered if he was with me, watching me. He'd barely been around when he was alive, weird to think he cared about me now that he was dead.

An old man, bow-legged, walked off the path to a gravestone. He stood above it, then held his head in his hands. His shoulders shook with sobs. I watched him with envy, wishing I could do that, let go. But it was too late. Whatever emotions had been inside me had turned hard, cooked by the meth.

HOPE

"Where are you going?" Cassie asked sleepily as I put on my slippers.

"I have to pee," I whispered. She rolled over and faced the wall. The branch outside the window rapped on the glass, disputing my lie. *Shut up.*

I closed the door carefully and snuck down the hallway. If Ms. Harrison caught me out of my room at midnight, I'd get detention. If she found us drinking, it would be worse. I had to admit, tiptoeing down the hallway, that this was thrilling. My heart beat quickly with trepidation as I went past Ms. Harrison's room.

I knocked softly on Lizzie's door and heard a giggle. "Get in here," she whispered, peeking down the hallway. I was barely inside before she'd shut the door. Emily and Vivian were sitting on the floor and gave me conspiratorial grins.

"Vivian just came up with the best idea," Lizzie started in a hushed voice. She leaned in with a giddy smile. With rosy cheeks and wide, shining eyes, she looked like a wholesome schoolgirl. But, when she put her face close to mine, I could smell her breath. The sweet tang of alcohol, something sugary, enveloped me. It wasn't wholesomeness that had made her eyes shine, it was booze.

"Here." Emily reached behind her and pulled out a bottle. Vodka, probably, peach flavoured to make it drinkable. She waved it under my nose. It smelled like candy.

"That's okay. I don't want any," I said, shaking my head.

"Oh, come on!" Lizzie hissed. "Just a sip. No one's going to tell on you." I watched each girl warily. They hadn't drunk enough to be unruly, but there was an air of recklessness that set me on edge. My stomach clenched at what would happen if they—we—got caught.

Even though all my instincts told me not to, I grabbed the bottle from Emily. Squeezing my eyes shut, I tipped it back and felt the alcohol burn down my throat. The sweet aftertaste of peach clung to my lips. "So, what's the idea?" I said changing the subject and passing the bottle to Vivian.

She looked around at us. "A drinking game: Truth or Dare." As if she'd invented it.

"Hope has to go first, she's new," Lizzie commanded, then giggled, resting her head on Emily's shoulder, who patted her cheek affectionately.

"That's not fair, she just got here." Vivian shook her head. "Emily, you go first."

I threw Vivian a grateful smile and sat down between her and Lizzie. Their room had the same furniture as mine and Cassie's. But instead of the bare-chested actors gracing the wall on Cassie's side of the bed, pictures cut out from fashion magazines had been taped up. Girls in sunglasses and huge purses boarding airplanes, the sun bathing them in a golden glow, or lying in grassy meadows wearing shimmering white dresses.

"Fine," Emily sighed. "Dare."

Vivian reached under the bed and pulled out two paper shopping bags. One had "Dare" written on it and the other "Truth." She held the "Dare" bag out to Emily, grinning with anticipation. Emily stuck her hand in and pulled out a slip of paper. Unfurling it, she read, "Strip naked and walk past Ms. Harrison's door three times."

We all squealed, Emily with wide-eyed dread. "Oh my God! I can't!" she wailed, laughing and crying at the same time.

"You have to!" Lizzie said.

I cringed for her and didn't think she'd do it, but before I knew it, her pajamas lay in a pile on the floor, and her round, white butt was at the door. It creaked when she opened it. We peered out as she tiptoed past Ms. Harrison's door, halfway down the hallway. Clamping a hand over my mouth, I watched as she walked once, twice, and then three times past the door. On the way back to the room, she dashed in, pushing us out of the way, stifling triumphant giggles.

We all collapsed onto the floor and Emily wagged the bottle in Lizzie's face. "Drink up!"

Lizzie volunteered to go next. She dug into the "Truth" bag. "What is your biggest fear?" Everyone got quiet. The warmth of the vodka had worked its way to my head. Things felt a little fuzzier. "Turning out like my mother."

Vivian and Emily each took a swig and the bottle came to me.

"Why?" I asked.

She pursed her lips, sobering up. "She killed herself."

I caught my breath and wished I hadn't asked. "Sorry," I mumbled. "I didn't know." The others exchanged glances and the mood in the room changed. I felt like an idiot for asking. This time, I drank without complaint.

Vivian picked a dare and had to text a topless photo of herself to one of their friends at Melton Prep.

I gaped as she pulled off her shirt and pushed her breasts together, covered them with an arm, and snapped a selfie, making sure her face wasn't in the shot, giggling as she pressed Send. "That one was easy," Emily chided her. "You do it all the time!"

We all took a drink. It was my turn. There was no way I could do one of the dares. "Truth," I said and took a deep breath as I reached into the bag. "The secret you don't want anyone to know."

I looked at all of them, my heart clenched at the thought of Eric.

I had to tell them. It was the game. The alcohol made my head light and warmth spread up from my throat. Lizzie's eyes bored into me.

I forced the words to leave my lips. "My brother's a meth addict." My chin quivered, waiting for their reaction.

"Are you kidding?" Emily asked, frowning.

"Look at her face," Vivian replied for me. "Either she's an amazing actress, or it's the truth." She reached out and held my hand.

"Have you ever tried it?" Lizzie asked, her eyes narrowed, like she could discern the truth with a penetrating gaze.

"Hey, only one question allowed," Emily said, playfully slapping Lizzie's arm. But the glance Emily received made it clear that Lizzie could change the rules if she wanted.

I shook my head. "No." I'd seen what it had done to my brother.

"That stuff's deadly." Lizzie stared at me, waiting for a reaction. Vivian squeezed my hand and then let go.

Lizzie glanced at the clock. "It's late." She took the bottle and twisted the cap back on. The game was over. "See you tomorrow," she said as Vivian and I slipped back into the hallway to go to our rooms.

Vivian gave me a silent wave and we went our separate ways. I fell asleep worried that I shouldn't have told them the shameful truth about Eric. I felt lighter without the dark shadow looming over my life. But, what if they told other people? Being the sister of a meth addict was the identity I'd tried to leave behind.

A secret
Held close
spills,
dripping like blood into
your waiting hands.

ERIC

I met Cheez in his basement, tossing my jacket onto the floor beside the couch. He had all the supplies ready to go. Spread out like a crystal-meth buffet. About a year ago, he'd given me my first hit, looking for someone to party with. It was a slippery slope. Pretty soon, I was hanging around outside his house, waiting for him to come home from work.

He was careful, only shooting crystal on weekends, so he could crash the next day. I'd learned his schedule. Lots of times, he bought enough for both of us. If I had cash on me, I'd pay him back, but he was cool if I couldn't quite cover it. Cheez was a good guy.

I passed Cheez a handful of change. Added up to ten dollars. I'd panhandled all day by the gas station, breathing in the fumes, so I wouldn't come empty-handed. He took it and snorted. "That all you got?"

Rolling up my sleeve, I could almost taste the speed. My teeth ached with want of it. "I can get more next time, man. How much do you want?"

"You owe me twenty from last weekend and another

thirty from the week before. Shit, Eric. If you can't pay up …" He shook his head.

I rocked back and forth, the threat potent, staring at the bag of crank on the table. Like shards of ice, beautiful and sharp. "Okay, okay. I'm good for it, I fucking promise, I swear!"

"Yeah, well, that new jacket of yours must have cost a few bills."

"That was a gift." He was right, though. Selling it would bring in enough money to get high for a couple of weeks. "My sister." He'd turned on some music, something heavy, the bass pounding out of his speakers. "If I had any more, I'd give it to you, you know that. What about that job you were talking about, working for the town, doing landscaping and shit? That still gonna happen?"

He threw me a disgusted look. "I told you about that months ago, at the beginning of summer. You didn't do anything about it?"

I scratched my head. Months? It felt like last week.

"It was a summer job. Summer's over. Fuck, man. You're getting too into this shit." He flopped back onto the couch. We still hadn't taken a hit, and having it within arm's reach was torture. I leaned toward it, to let him know I was ready, but he started talking again.

"There might be some winter work, snow removal, flooding outdoor rinks. You want me to ask around for you?"

"Yeah, yeah. That'd be good. I mean, I know about ice, right?"

He grunted in agreement. He started to roll up his sleeve, resting his elbow on his knee and tying off a vein.

Finally. I smiled with relief. If he'd talked a minute longer, I'd have punched him. "This is the last time. If you don't come with money next time, I'm not partying with you." He meant it. His eyes were arrows, shooting my way.

For a second, before the meth carried me away, I thought about what would happen if I didn't bring him the cash. I couldn't imagine not getting high. It was the only thing I looked forward to. It was the reason I woke up in the morning.

Without meth, what would be the point in living?

HOPE

I squirmed on the couch beside Vivian. "You know for sure it was Cassie?"

Lizzie shot me a piercing look. "Yes. It has to be. She probably told her brother and now it's all over Melton. She's *always* hated me."

"She's just jealous of you," Emily muttered, tufts of downy curls framing her face.

"And a complete bitch," Lizzie fumed, her red lips pulled into a scowl. "Girls like her *look* harmless. You should be careful." She turned to me. "You never know what she's saying behind your back."

Across the room, Cassie and another girl sat with their heads together, avoiding looking in our direction. She'd asked a few times what I talked about with Lizzie, Vivian, and Emily, digging for details and turning away in a huff when I wouldn't tell her. Things had gotten chillier between Cassie and me since I started sitting with Lizzie and her friends at lunch and in the common room.

I looked longingly at some of the other girls, laughing together, relaxed. Everything with Lizzie was a drama, there was no letting your guard down. But at least I had someone to sit with. Cassie had never invited me to spend time with her friends.

"I have never given any Meltie a blow job," Lizzie explained, using the nickname for boys who went to Melton Prep. Vivian and Emily shook their heads. "And she's making it sound like I went down on half of the grade twelves."

"Why do you think it was Cassie who started the rumour?" I asked.

She rounded on me. "Are you defending her?"

I cringed in my seat, wishing I was somewhere else. "No. I just want to know who started it."

Lizzie glared at me. "I told you who it was. She goes out of her way to make me look bad. If you'd rather be friends with that fat cow, go ahead. But I can't even look at her," Lizzie said loudly. "She's a backstabbing bitch." A noticeable hush fell over the room as Lizzie stalked off. Cassie looked as confused as everyone else.

"Do you think Cassie really said those things?" I asked Vivian.

She leaned in conspiratorially. "She and Lizzie have never gotten along." I wrinkled my forehead, waiting for more. "It's because Lizzie had a thing for Cassie's brother. He's, like, one of the best-looking guys at Melton. But," she dropped her voice, "he won't even talk to Lizzie. She thinks it's because of Cassie."

Was that why Cassie had warned me about Lizzie, because of a feud over her brother? "Why is it such a big deal?"

Vivian shrugged. "Lizzie gets like that," she sighed. "Cassie and I used to be friends, but Lizzie made me choose. Said I couldn't be friends with her if I was friends with Cassie. Sometimes I think it's just a game to her, seeing if we'll do what she wants us to." Vivian's phone buzzed with a text. She grew quiet as she read it and then turned to me. "Lizzie wants to meet in her room tonight. She says she has a plan for—" She chin-nodded toward Cassie.

"A plan?"

Vivian shrugged. "Sometimes it's easier to just go along with things."

"Yeah," I said, like it made sense to me. I didn't get their inside jokes or understand their secret code of girl behaviour, but I didn't want to spend the next four years alone. I wanted things to be different at Ravenhurst. It wasn't Lumsville; Eric wasn't here, a shadow I couldn't shake off. Anyhow, what was the worst Lizzie could do?

ERIC

I had a girlfriend, before, when I was playing hockey. Christa. Now she works at the grocery store in town, saving up to go to university. Light brown hair, cute. She'd come to my games and watch in the corner, too nervous to sit with the other fans. We used to mess around in her parents' basement. Didn't get too far with her, though. She was a good girl.

I saw her through the window standing at the checkout. Her hands moved automatically, sweeping things over the scanner. Keeping my head down, I ducked inside. I hadn't seen her in months, maybe longer.

The shelves were full of cans and boxes, the labels bright. They lit up the aisles like fireworks. I wanted to take one of everything, but I couldn't fit it all in my arms. Things started to tumble out, spilling to the floor and making a fucking racket. "Shh!" I hissed at the groceries. I had to walk away, leaving the pile in the middle of the aisle. The sound of the cans banging on the floor echoed in my head. I darted down an aisle and grabbed some bread. Squeezing it, the cellophane bag rustled in my hands. I wanted to rip it open and sink my teeth into the spongey softness.

When I got into Christa's line, she looked up at me, her face flickering recognition, then a frown, one eyebrow crunching against the other one. *You look good*, I wanted to tell her. But she looked uncomfortable, like I'd said something rude, when I hadn't even opened my mouth yet.

I flashed her a grin. Good thing I was buzzing on meth, otherwise, it could be awkward, seeing her after so long. I dumped the loaf of bread and a couple of cans of ravioli I'd rescued from an aisle display onto the conveyor belt. Someone got into line after me, but she held up her closed sign. "Sorry," she said to the guy behind me. "He's my last customer."

She held her finger over the bar code on each item and put them into a bag. The total on the computer screen didn't change from zero. She didn't have to help me, but she was. My gratitude spilled over in disjointed conversation about the weather, school, hockey. I spoke too fast, words spilling out.

"Thanks, Christa," I said, eager to grab the bag. Our hands collided. She pulled hers away quickly, like from a too-hot pan. Flustered, she looked away, tidying the stack of bags at her till. "See you around."

She nodded. Through the window, I waved to her, bursting with gratitude. But she wasn't looking at me. She was leaning against the cash register, her forehead in her hands.

HOPE

The four of us were sitting in a circle on the floor. I was relieved to see that no bottle was being passed around tonight. But the look of anticipation on Lizzie's face meant she had something else brewing.

"I came up with a plan," Lizzie said. From behind her back, she pulled out a pair of scissors. "Guess what you have to do." Her mouth twitched with eagerness.

I shook my head.

"Cut Cassie's hair."

My mouth went slack as I stared at them in disbelief. "Her hair?" I thought of her golden curls, ringlets that hung halfway down her back.

"Tonight!" The excitement in her voice made my stomach queasy.

I looked at Vivian and Emily, as shocked as I was. "You're joking." Lizzie pressed the scissors into my hand. Heavy and metal, with a long blade, they sat cold on my palm.

Lizzie's eyes bored through me. "You have to. After what she did to me, she deserves it. You think so, right?

That she can't get away with spreading rumours, saying horrible things about me."

A tinge of distrust for Lizzie bit back at me. It was too much, what she was asking me to do. She must have seen the doubt in my face.

She sat back and fixed me with a hard look. "If you want us to stay friends, you'll do it."

Vivian's eyes darted to Lizzie. She'd been in the same positon as I was. I waited for her to say something, but she stayed quiet. She and Emily, their silence meant solidarity with Lizzie. They stared back at me. Three against one.

The scissors lay in my hand. I stood up and took a few shaky steps backwards, inching toward the door. "I better go," I mumbled. Their eyes lit up and they grinned victoriously at one another. "Bring us some! After you do it, bring me some hair," Lizzie whispered after me. I walked with the scissors pressed against my thigh, the chill of the metal making me shiver.

Cassie was sound asleep, her snores filling the room. In the darkness, I could make out the outline of her hair running like liquid gold over her pillow.

Standing by the door, I didn't trust myself to go any closer.

I thought about snipping a chunk from underneath, something she'd never miss, but that wasn't what they were after. They wanted her shorn, her angelic tresses lopped off for all to see. I took a step closer. The floor creaked under me. Cassie snorted and turned over, her face to the wall, exposing her full head of hair to me. Now was my chance. I moved my fingers into the handles and opened the blades; they scraped against one another, metal to metal. Her hair was within arm's length. I just had to reach out, grab a huge handful, and hack through it with the scissors. If I was gentle, she might not even wake up.

But she'd know it was me. Who else could have come into our room and butchered her hair? But was it any stranger than the truth? That I was doing it because Lizzie had commanded me to?

A cold sweat broke out over my forehead and a chill ran up my neck, as if I was about to throw up. I reached a finger out to touch a tendril of her hair. The silky soft curl wound itself around my finger.

Closing my eyes, I thought about what I was doing: standing in a dark room, holding scissors to my roommate's hair, ready to chop it off. It was ludicrous. This was not who I was. With a cry of revulsion, I stormed across the room, slammed the scissors onto my desk and opened the window. The scissors gleamed in the darkness, one blade shining. Picking them up, I hurled them out the window.

"Hope?" Cassie called from her bed. "What're you doin?" she mumbled.

"Nothing," I said and shut the window. "I'm not doing anything."

I would lie tomorrow when they saw Cassie. I'd say the timing hadn't been right, that she was a light sleeper and had woken up when I came into the room.

Or tell them the truth, that it was an unfair punishment. Cutting her hair as payback for a rumour didn't make sense.

They'd think I'd chosen sides, picked Cassie over them. I guess, in a way, I had. But it was the right choice. How could I have lived with myself if I'd done it?

ERIC

The neon green cross in the pharmacy window flickered. I'd been sitting on the curb across the street for the last forty-five minutes, waiting. For what, I didn't know.

Guts? Desperation?

There'd be good shit inside. Things I could sell, and a cash register or safe. I'd seen robberies on TV, the police shows my stepdad liked to watch. How hard could it be? No one was inside to get hurt. I just had to go in, grab what I needed, and take off.

I'd begged Joanne at the truck stop on Highway 9 for a coffee. I think she'd dated my dad in high school and felt bad when she saw me, remembering him. She said we looked a lot alike. "Good-looking?" I'd asked her one time, but she'd just laughed and touched my arm.

Today, she'd shooed me away from the counter "We're getting slammed," she'd said, breathless. "Dinner rush."

"Please?" I cajoled.

She must have figured the only way I'd leave was if she gave in. "Fine. I'll bring you a coffee out back in ten minutes."

Now I was hyped up on coffee and the nine packs of sugar I'd dumped into it. My feet rattled on the pavement. It felt like bugs were crawling through my skin, up my toes, spiralling around my legs, scampering across my balls, and then racing up my stomach till they settled in my brain, nesting there. Waiting.

I moaned. I needed a fix something bad. Cheez wouldn't spot me any crank unless I came back with some cash. So that was what I was doing. Figuring it out, my way.

The back door of the pharmacy was in an alley. It had an alarm. There was a sticker on the door. And a deadbolt and who knew what else. The glass on the door had bars, but there was another window, partly blocked by a cooler, and it had no bars.

If I broke the window and climbed over the cooler, I could squeeze in. Never could have fit when I was playing hockey. Months of meth had made me lean.

I had to do it now, before stuff started to make sense.

Taking off my jacket, I left it by the building, out of sight but easy to grab when I took off. I picked up a brick, the rough edges scraped my fingers, ripping fingernails.

I slammed the brick against the window once. Not even a dent. I looked around. No one in sight. I raised it again and whacked it harder. Somewhere, a dog barked.

Fucking tempered glass. It took two more whacks until a crack splintered the glass. A trickle of sweat ran down my back. Another hit and the whole bottom corner shattered into cubes at my feet. I shielded my eyes and tossed the brick behind me. The whole window collapsed and an alarm started ringing. Standing on the window ledge, I hauled myself up and over the cooler. The space was narrow—my spine scraped against the top of the window sill, jagged bits of glass embedding themselves in my skin—but I wiggled through, sinewy ropes of muscle flexing in my arms. I dropped down on the other side and ran to the counter.

Fuck me. There was a metal screen pulled down in front of the counter. Had I known about that? I should have had a plan, but with the alarm screaming, I couldn't focus. With a frustrated yell, I tossed bottles of mouthwash and toothpaste against the screen. They bounced back into the aisle, doing nothing to the screen except making it rattle. I swept whole shelves of stuff down to the floor, spinning around, trashing the place.

I ran to the first-aid aisle. I'd grab some bottles of pain relievers, as many as I could carry. At least I could sell them on the street. It didn't matter what kind of drug you had, someone would want it. The pockets on my shorts were deep; front and back bulged with containers of pills.

I grabbed some rubbing alcohol and bandages. My back had started to sting and my hands had blood on them, I didn't know from what. I must have cut myself on the broken window glass. Hauling ass to the door, I unlocked it, grabbed my jacket, and ran across the parking lot to the other side of the street. No one was around, but there wasn't any cover either. I had to get to the highway, try and hitch out of here.

I looked back once. The alarm still blared, but no one had shown up yet. The pharmacy was empty and damaged. A black hole.

Just like me.

HOPE

I lay awake all night, wondering what to do. At breakfast, they'd be looking for me. I'd have to explain why
Cassie still had long hair. That I'd chosen to protect her
over backing up my friends.

By the time morning came, my stomach was churning. There was no way I could face them.

I watched from my bed as Cassie fluffed her hair,
scrunching the curls with her hands. They hung lustrous
against her navy sweater. "Want me to get you some
toast?" she asked.

I shook my head. "No, thanks. I'm not hungry."

"Hope you feel better," she said and gave me a sym-
pathetic smile. "I'll leave a note on Ms. Harrison's door,
so she knows you're sick. She'll tell the teachers."

I nodded gratefully, clutching my stomach. "Probably just cramps."

With a nod, she disappeared out the door.

It was better to stay out of sight today. Let the
Ravens notice Cassie's hair without me being around.
Now that the morning sun was trickling through the
windows, last night felt like a hallucination. I wanted to

believe that the whole thing had been a joke, something they hadn't meant for me to actually do, but I couldn't be sure. I'd held the scissors in my hand. I'd thought about it. That was the part that disgusted me: I'd *considered* it.

The blackbird landed on his perch. He opened his beak and let loose a loud "*Caw!*" A judgment.

"Shut up," I whispered at him.

Shattered words and ideas floated in my head. I wanted to write something, find a vent for what was going on in my head.

I grabbed my journal and a pen from my nightstand drawer.

> Wicked lies
> Burn bright
> In the night sky.

Just writing the words felt better, some proof that the old me hadn't completely disappeared.

ERIC

I stayed hidden in the scrub by the side of the road. It was dry; the grass prickled and bit at me. I'd have to thumb a ride to the city, somewhere I could get lost.

I imagined what Hope would do when I showed up at her school. And then stopped. I was sober enough to remember who I was. Not the hockey player, not the guy who people wanted to be friends with, who they looked up to.

I was a junkie.

What if she turned away from me, embarrassed? I couldn't take that, not from her. In my head, I was still the older brother, the one who was supposed to look out for her.

A semi drove past, kicking up a whirlwind of dust. It flew in my eyes and nose, making me cough. My chest rattled. There was a scab on my hand and I started to pick at it. Fresh, red blood seeped out. There wasn't any new skin yet, just a raw wound.

Maybe getting to the city wasn't the end of the line for me. I could go farther, out West, where the weather was better. Maybe to the ocean. My mind reeled with plans, unfurling like a ribbon in front of me.

For now, though, I'd go to the city. Find Hope. If she had any money, she'd give it to me. She'd know I needed it more than she did.

The sky was getting lighter, pinker, as the sun rose. I moved to the shoulder of the road and stuck out my thumb. I was travelling light. No backpack, only pockets swollen with what I had stolen at the pharmacy. I hadn't checked how deep the cuts on my back were, but they stung every time I moved. My shirt stuck to the dried blood, pulling at the wounds.

Another semi approached and blew past me. I ducked my head to my chest, shutting my eyes against the dust. Same thing with the next two, but then one put on his signal and pulled over, rumbling to a stop on the gravel.

I ran over, the pills rattling in my pockets. "You going to the city?" I asked.

The driver leaned out the window. He had a few days' worth of stubble on him and bristly brown hair. He was flabby and nondescript. "I can drop you off at the perimeter."

I ran around to the passenger side and climbed up. The cab was dusty, with trinkets and trash all over the seat and floor. Pictures of the guy's kids were stuffed into the corners of the windshield. They were old and faded. Those kids could be in their twenties by now, but they were seven and nine forever in the truck.

"Been driving all night. Be good to have someone to talk to. I'm Mike."

I hesitated, not wanting to give him my real name. "Darren," I said, after my favourite hockey player, Darren Risk. A small-town boy, he went first round in the draft pick to the Habs. That could have been me, if things hadn't gone sideways.

"Got some coffee in the Thermos, if you want some." He nodded to the back where his mattress lay, the sheets unrumpled.

I was going to say no, but then I thought, what the hell? He'd offered and I didn't know when my next meal was coming. I had to start thinking smart, taking hand-outs when they came. That was the way to survive.

Mike didn't ask me too much personal stuff. I started to relax and watch the empty expanse go past, zoning out, then sleeping.

"Hey," he said shaking me awake. His coffee breath hit me and I looked the other way.

"We here?" I asked. We were stopped. Outside the window, a gas station sat at the other side of a parking lot.

Mike shook his head and snorted. I got the feeling he wasn't real happy with me. "Shoulda known better than to pick up a junkie."

He looked at me hungrily. There was a coldness in his eyes that didn't fit with the guy who'd offered me some of his coffee a couple of hours ago, the guy who had pictures of his kids on his dash.

I felt my heart thud, heavy in my chest. Nothing felt right anymore. I needed to get out of his truck. The door was locked.

"Where you going?" he asked. "You think a ride doesn't cost anything?"

He leered at me and started unbuckling his belt. Bitter, acidic coffee rose up in my throat. I'd puke on him if he made me suck him.

"Come on. Don't be like that. You wanted the ride."

Fuck. I started to cry, holding my stomach and whimpering. I couldn't do this again.

"It's okay," he soothed me, resting a hand on my shoulder. "It'll be over soon and I'll drop you off. Anywhere you want."

My stomach heaved. I gripped the door handle, but it didn't budge. I was trapped.

"Come on, *Darren*," he said with a moan of anticipation. "There's only one way you're getting out of here."

I heard him unzip his pants but couldn't look. The metal teeth unhooking themselves from each other, separating, dividing like a fault line.

He grabbed the back of my neck, pulling me down. I struggled against him and then gave up. What was the point? He'd get it one way or the other.

Sticking my face into that dank, foul place, I caught my gag reflex in time and slipped into darkness. To a place where I didn't have to think, where I could disappear.

"Ah, yeah," Mike exhaled, twisting his hand into my hair. He gave a soft laugh. "This isn't your first time, is it?"

HOPE

I stood on tiptoes, rereading my words.

> The ravens swoop
> Attack with beady yellow eyes
> A cackle of greeting
> For their prey.
> A murder,
> They find each other.
> There are no innocents.

Stepping down from the chair, the poem disappeared. Tiny letters on the wall above the door frame. Indiscernible to anyone else's eye, but I'd know they were there. Every time I walked under them. The same poem sandwiched in my journal, a fragment of me.

I'd delayed leaving my room for as long as I could. Cassie had sneaked food upstairs for me the day before, but Ms. Harrison would make me visit the infirmary if I missed another day of school. Waiting until the last possible moment, I raced to the dining hall and grabbed a piece of toast. I didn't sit to eat it, there was no time.

Instead, I kept my head down and stuffed it into my mouth as I walked to class.

I could feel Lizzie's narrowed-eye glare as I slid into my seat.

"Where were you?" she hissed across the aisle.

"Not feeling well," I whispered back, barely turning my head. I watched impatiently as one of the girls monopolized Ms. Tate's attention. I wanted her to start the lesson so I could avoid Lizzie's questions. I opened my binder. Blank pages stared back at me. Poems simmered in my head. Picking up my pen, I was about to write something, but Lizzie's insistent whisper came at me again.

"Why didn't you do it?"

"I just couldn't." I caught myself before adding an apology. I wasn't sorry.

"A real friend would have done it."

I glanced over at Cassie, imagining her hair shorn, hacked to nothing, like a field of stubbly wheat stalks. The image of her waking up, seeing dead strands of her hair littered on the pillow, the sheets, the floor, how she'd scream, made me shiver.

I looked at Lizzie. She was such a private school cliché. I'd be better off with no friends than ones like the Ravens. "A real friend wouldn't have asked me," I fired back at her, shocked at the venom in my words.

She gave me a wicked smile. "I was never your friend."

I stared so hard at the lines on my paper, they blurred.

Ms. Tate was saying something. I focused on her, ignoring Lizzie. My pen slipped and rolled to the floor.

In one brutal motion, Lizzie scooped it up, snapped it in half, and tossed it back at me. Ink leaked out, a blue blood bath seeping across my desk.

ERIC

It started to rain. Huge drops that soaked my shirt, making me shiver. Mike had left me under a sign welcoming visitors to the city. The skyline lay ahead of me, shrouded in grey cloud. Everything felt foggy. I kept getting Mike confused with Coach Williams, my brain playing tricks on me.

Mike could have beaten me, or done worse. But the taste of him in my mouth made me retch.

I started scratching my hand again, the newly formed scab still soft and pliable. It peeled off, blood rushed to the surface. Mixing with the rain, it ran down my fingers in rivulets.

Cars zipped by, dousing me with spray, their wheels spinning as they raced down the highway. I wouldn't hitch again. My steps wobbled, weaving onto the road and back to the shoulder. A car honked, its horn blaring, scaring the shit out of me and making me jump out of the way, back to the shoulder. I stood there shuddering, my nerves shot.

A box lay in the ditch, wiggling. What the fuck? I blinked, wiped the rain out of my eyes and took another look.

It was wet and folded down on itself, the cardboard soaked, but it was rocking, almost tipping over. I slid down into the tall grass. Puddles of fetid water sucked at my feet as I crossed to the box. Inside was a dog. A small, black puppy with pointed ears and a snout speckled with white. He started whimpering, brown eyes still half-closed with newness.

I put my hand into the box. The dog sniffed, curious, too young to be scared. A little pink tongue shot out, rough and warm, licking my fingers, drinking the raindrops.

"You're hungry," I said out loud. I had no food for myself, never mind the dog. Could he drink ditch water? I wrapped my hands around his middle. Wet and skinny, his heart beat like crazy and he tried to scramble out of my hands.

"Shush, shush," I soothed him, holding him against me. His paws scratched me, but I patted his head, the skull impossibly small under my fingers. How old was he? A few weeks? Tossed onto the roadside to die. Whoever did it should have just killed him, not left him to starve.

The dog calmed down, nestled against my chest. Tucked himself into my jacket. A bit farther up was a truck stop. They might not want to give me food, but a helpless puppy?

Exhaust fumes belched at me as I crossed the parking lot. The asphalt was slick with rain. One of my shoelaces had come undone, but I couldn't bend down to tie it, in case the puppy ran off. I needed to find something for a leash so I could keep him with me.

The guy at the till looked me up and down when I walked in. "No dogs," he said catching sight of the one in my arms.

"He's a puppy. I found him in the ditch." I tried to push his head towards the guy at the counter so he could see how helpless the dog was.

"Don't care," he growled. I looked around at the perfectly stocked shelves, bright drinks glowing in the coolers, racks of shiny magazines, and the rotating corn dog display.

"Come on, man. You can't help me out? I just want some food for the dog."

His face stayed blank. Did he want me to beg?

"This place is a fucking rip-off anyway." I kicked the door open. I didn't care if the other customers stared at me. I stumbled back outside, into the rain. I'd take my chances in the garbage, or keep walking until I found someone who wasn't a heartless bastard.

A frayed pink rope lay beside bundles of firewood for sale. I picked it up and wrapped it around the dog's neck, but it was too loose and he slipped his head out of it. "Don't like being tied up, do you?" Tossing the rope away, I remembered the gauze I'd taken from the pharmacy, first aid for my hands. It seemed like so long ago that I'd left Lumsville, but it had only been hours.

Damp from the rain, the gauze stretched and stuck to the dog's fur so he couldn't wriggle out of it. When I put the dog on the ground, he skittered away, not sure what to do, and then lay down, pawing at the leash.

I took a minute to look around. Another stretch of highway led into the city. The downtown skyline loomed in the distance. If I made it there, I'd be able to find food and a place to crash.

I wasn't just thinking of me anymore. I had a dog to look after.

If I got the city, I could find Hope. She'd help me. I just had to remember the name of her school. My brain was fried.

And the dog. It needed a name. I bent down again and checked, lifting a paw against his wishes. A girl.

Rain dripped from my forehead onto my lips. I licked it away. Fresh. A paper cup rolled across the pavement toward us. I ripped off the top half and let the water collect in it so she could drink. My jacket's odour, pungent wet leather, musky, reminded me of my hockey gear. The smell trapped in the bag, released when I opened it. But I pushed those thoughts away. I'd left that world behind. I was here now, lost on a highway. Better than being stuck in Lumsville.

I smiled as the dog's pink tongue darted out to lap the water up. She needed a tough name, something nobody would mess with.

Storm.

"Come on, Stormy," I tried. It sounded right.

I wrapped the gauze around my fingers and started walking. I wasn't as tired anymore, or as dazed. The rain and Storm had brought me back around. As long as I could find Hope, I'd be okay.

HOPE

I'd been avoiding Lizzie, Vivian, and Emily. There were no more invitations to sit with them in the common room or dining hall. Instead, they dipped into whispered conversations when they saw me, Lizzie and Emily throwing cold looks my way. And Vivian, frowning with disappointment. Their new recruit had failed.

"You were right about those girls being a prickly bunch," I said to Cassie as we got ready for bed. My hair was still wet from a late-night shower and hung in long clumps down my back. I was looking for sympathy from her, maybe an invitation to join her friends at breakfast tomorrow. She ignored me.

"Cassie? What's wrong?"

Crawling into bed, she punched her pillow and looked at me with watery blue eyes. "I know what you've been saying behind my back."

I stared at her, confused. I hadn't said anything about her.

"You told Vivian you heard me talking to my brother, telling him lies about Lizzie, about how many guys she's been with," she accused. "Which is a total lie, because Parker and I don't talk on the phone. We only text!"

I froze, paralyzed by her words. "Vivian told you that?"

"Yeah, she wanted me to know what a backstabber you are. I guess you'll do anything to get in with them, won't you? Even spread lies about your roommate." Cassie's eyes bulged at me, her cheeks flaming red.

Shaking my head, I tried to argue with her, my chest tightening with frustration, the need for her to believe me. "I swear, Cassie, none of that is true! They flipped everything around to make me look like the bad guy."

She just snorted with disgust at me. I almost blurted out the truth, that I'd stood over her with scissors, on the Ravens' orders, willing to cut her hair to satisfy them. But that made me sound even less trustworthy.

I was ashamed I'd even thought about doing it.

"Cassie?" I wanted to explain, but she wouldn't look at me. It was like talking to a statue.

The Ravens had turned on me. I'd gone from their inner circle to their enemy in two days. They'd also managed to turn Cassie against me. I rolled over in bed and stared at the wall. Tears collected in my eyes and tumbled out onto the pillow. I'd only been looking for friends, for someone to spend my time with. Instead, I'd gotten so tangled up in drama, I didn't know how to find my way out.

In the dim light of the room, I searched for a pen.

Coiling under my skin
A viper waits to strike

Poisoned fangs
Bared.
For now
I sit alone
Waiting
Hoping it won't
Bite me first.

The words scrolled across my arm before I realized what I'd done. I stared at them, loving the way they snaked down to my wrist, the sting on my skin from the pressure of the pen. A hurt that matched how I felt on the inside.

My body, paper, walls, sheets, furniture: my poems could mark them all.

ERIC

A church. They'd help. Didn't they have to? I let Storm down. The rain had almost stopped—just a light drizzle sprinkled us, pinging in the puddles. Storm zigzagged around the grass, sometimes losing her footing and sliding down but then scrambling back up.

Church was a big deal in Lumsville. Not for our family, though. Mom had stopped going, even though her parents were big Bible-thumpers. Maybe that was why she married my dad so young. Wanted to rebel. Kids at school used to tell me I was going to hell because we didn't go to church, but once I got good at hockey, that all stopped. Maybe hockey players got into heaven no matter what.

There were two cars in the parking lot, but the front doors were locked. I went around to a side door marked OFFICE. A lady with grey hair and glasses, who looked like the best grandma anyone could want, spun around in her rolling office chair when I walked in.

She did a double take, blinking away her shock at my arrival. "Can I help you, dear?" She said *dear* like an afterthought.

Storm twisted in my arms, nipping at my chin. "Sorry to bother you," I began, not even sure what to say. "I found this dog and she's real little, just a couple weeks old. I wondered if you had something for her to drink, some milk or something." I huddled farther into my jacket, soaked and heavy. "I'm real hungry too, but it's no problem if you just want to feed the dog. She's what I'm worried about."

"Oh my." The lady raised her eyebrows and looked at Storm. "Poor thing. Wait here and I'll see if we have anything in the kitchen."

I nodded, conscious of the wet spot I'd made on the carpet. I started to shiver too, now that I was inside and standing still. Storm kept licking the rain off my neck.

There was church music playing. A choir singing sombre notes. She came back with a Styrofoam cup of steaming water and a tea bag bobbing on the surface. In her other hand was a bowl of cream. I was at least two feet taller than her and crouched down to take the tea from her hands, which were mottled with veins. They shook a little, but I think it was 'cause she was old, not because I scared her.

Storm sniffed the cream and then took a few licks.

"Here are some cookies, dear," the lady said. The sandwich kind with icing that matches the colour of the biscuit part. She'd put them on a hard plastic tray in an overlapping row. I wanted to stuff them all into my mouth, but I didn't. Even though my stomach was twisting itself in a knot because I was so hungry, I only took four and nodded my thanks, sliding the tray back onto her desk.

"My car broke down, a ways back. I'm trying to get to the city to see a friend of mine. Do you know about buses around here?"

If she knew I was lying, she didn't show it. "No, I don't. But we have a van coming to pick up some donations for a church downtown. I'm sure Albert would give you a ride to wherever you need to go. Or I could call you a tow truck?"

"A lift with that guy, Albert. That would be great. I'll deal with my car later." Relief washed over me. I looked at Storm, her tail wagging as she lapped up the cream. She was bringing me good luck.

For a second, a glimmer of doubt rose up. I'd be trapped alone in a car with a guy, some stranger I didn't know. What if he tried the same thing as Mike?

And then the self-hatred washed over me. My mind cartwheeled back in time, spinning through images like a merry-go-round in high gear. All the way back to the road trip in Duluth. The first time. I couldn't handle the memories this clean. I needed a fix.

The fake sweet icing in the cookies coated my stomach, sticking like tar. Sitting here would kill me. The clock ticking by, her fingers clacking on computer keys. I'd get so agitated, I'd go ballistic.

"Actually, thanks, but I'll just head out on my own. Don't want to trouble you. Thanks," I babbled and scooped up Storm. A droplet of cream clung to her chin, caught in a stubbly whisker. The lady tried to get out of her chair, claiming it was no trouble, but I was already out the door. Happy to be breathing fresh air.

"Come on, Storm," I said to her, more of a whisper.

I could feel myself sinking. No meth for, what was it, twelve hours, maybe more? Thoughts of Coach Williams would swirl around me, squeezing me until I couldn't stand it anymore.

I needed something to feel good again.

The city was within reach. I just had to get there.

HOPE

I'd spent the day skirting the halls like a ghost. Lizzie, Emily, and Vivian had ignored me. Cassie had too, but worse, she'd told some of the other girls why she was mad at me. I had gotten evil glares in every class.

When I got back to my room at the end of the day, I tossed my books onto my desk and turned on my computer, hoping Mom had sent a message. Proof that someone was thinking about me.

I stared at the screen in surprise. Today, in bold print amid the junk mail, was a new message.

> Wednesday, September 10, 4:46 p.m.
> **To:** Hope Randall <hrandall@ravenhurst.ca>
> **From:** Devon Huddington
> <dhuddington@melton.ca>
> **Subject:** Hi
>
> My name is Devon, and I'm on the Melton-Ravenhurst Welcoming Committee. You probably figured out that Melton Preparatory Academy is the brother school to Ravenhurst. We check in with new students to make sure they're settling in okay and to see if they have any questions.

> Let me know if you need anything. Where
> were you before starting at RH? By the way, nice
> profile pic. You look good in your uniform. ☺
> Cheers,
> D.

Profile picture? I opened the Ravenhurst web-sites, entered my password, and clicked on "Student Directory." Sure enough, there was my student ID photo and contact information. I went to the Melton website and found Devon Huddington. He was cute. Like, really cute. Brown hair that flopped over his fore-head and warm, dark eyes. I found myself smiling as I typed a reply.

> Thursday, September 11, 9:10 p.m.
> **To:** Devon
> **From:** Hope
> **Re:** Hi
>
> Thanks for the email. I'm from Lumsville. It's a
> really small town, so don't worry if you've never
> heard of it. I guess I'm settling in okay. I've
> never boarded before, so it gets kind of lonely.
> Have you been at Melton a long time? Do you
> like it?
> Hope

I reread my email, frowning at the lie. *Settling in okay*. The truth was I'd never felt so alone in my life, but I couldn't admit that to someone I'd never met. Before I could overthink it, I pressed Send. A few minutes later, another email appeared.

Thursday, September 11, 9:23 p.m.
To: Hope
From: Devon
Re: Hi

I call the place Hellton. I started in grade
seven and I hate it. I'm from up north. Both
my parents are doctors and travel all over the
Territories for work, so I got dumped here.

The Welcome Committee actually doesn't
exist. I just wanted a reason to email you. Saw
your profile on the school directory and was
interested. ;-) Don't be mad at me.

I'm just sick of the stuck-up bitches who
go to your school.
D.

ERIC

I hadn't made it to the city yet. The skyline still clung to the horizon. Without meth energy, getting there felt impossible. But I'd come too far to do anything else.

We'd spent the night in the parking lot of an amusement park. Closed on weekdays, all the metal rides sat frozen, silent. But the garbage cans overflowed with things to eat: soggy plates of fries with congealed ketchup; half-eaten hot dogs rolled up like mummies in their foil wrappers; plastic containers with barely touched salads, the lettuce brown but edible; and bottles of pop, flat, but filled with sugary goodness. Wasps buzzed around the remnants of our meal, dive-bombing like fighter pilots. We'd gone to sleep last night with full bellies.

But now, the next morning, I needed a fix.

I needed to find Hope.

HOPE

My stomach dropped when I read Mom's email: "Call me ASAP." Why couldn't it just say "Everything's great here. Nothing to worry about"?

I held my phone in my hand and stared at it, willing myself to press her number. I didn't want any bad news and with an email like that, what else could it be?

It had to be about Eric. Something had happened to him. We all knew it was only a matter of time before we got a call from the hospital or the cops showed up at our door. He'd tried to hide that he was using at first, avoiding us and staying out all day, only coming home when he knew we'd be in bed. But I'd lie awake until I heard him open the front door and turn the TV on. Sometimes it would be 3:00 or 4:00 a.m. I'd breathe a sigh of relief knowing he was home safe and tiptoe past his bedroom in the morning, careful not to wake him. We all thought he was just partying, out with friends, celebrating the fact that hockey was done for the season.

This went on for weeks until Mom cornered him one day at breakfast. Dark circles ringed his eyes and he looked haunted, not like himself. He'd told her he was having trouble sleeping and stormed out of the house. He'd slammed the door so hard the glasses in the cupboards rattled.

I didn't tell Mom what I'd heard people saying at school. Shaking their heads at how low he'd sunk.

He appeared in my room one night, talking a mile a minute and pacing. He told me about his hockey games, reliving each one in detail. He wouldn't calm down. The energy in him was like a volcano, ready to explode. And he wouldn't look at me. It was like he was in his own world and I was stuck behind glass, watching him. "Eric!" I'd shouted. "What are you doing?" When he'd looked at me, his eyes were wide with shock that someone was in the room with him. He took off again, yelling that I'd ruined his life. I ran after him on newly thawed ground, the ice crystals cutting into my bare feet.

He didn't come back for days. We found out later that he'd stayed with a friend whose parents were out of town. He'd trashed their house. They wanted to press charges, but Dad talked them out of it.

The cops brought him home one night. He'd been wandering around downtown Lumsville. Muttering and kicking garbage cans over, or trying to. I crept downstairs at the sound of voices, cowering behind the spindles. Mom sat in her housecoat at the kitchen table, listening to the cops. Dad ran his hand through his hair, over and over, a nervous tic. When the police left, Eric went ballistic. He tossed the kitchen chairs to the ground and kicked the fridge. "I don't need any of you!" Eric shouted. "You think you know me, but you don't." And then he barrelled up to his room, racing past me on the stairs. I heard him moving furniture around in his room, playing music so loud the walls shook.

I got used to the pattern of behaviour. He'd disappear for days and then come home when the high started to wear off so he could crash. He'd sleep for two days straight and wake up ravenous. Then, he'd mope around the house or spend the day staring at the TV, like his best friend had died.

He didn't go to school anymore. None of us were surprised when the principal called, asking Mom and Dad for a meeting at school. Eric was failing his classes. He wasn't going to graduate.

Mom and Dad gave him an ultimatum: either straighten out or live somewhere else.

I left my first poem for him taped to his door, where he'd be sure to see it.

> Sand running through
> My fingers.
> Fluid.
> I lost you in the cracks.
> I keep digging,
> But you are too
> Far
> Gone.

I don't know what he did with it, but when I came home from school that day, it was gone. And so was he.

ERIC

I pulled out the wad of papers in my back pocket. Hope's poems, eight of them folded together into a tight, thick package, and the photos she'd left for me. A couple I'd tossed, but the ones of us when we were kids, I kept.

I stared at the one of me in my hockey gear, grinning into the camera and leaning in a hockey stance on my stick.

I remembered that day. After the photos, Coach Williams had introduced himself. He'd seen me play and wanted me to come out for a few practices with the Hornets. A Junior AAA team. I'd bit back a smile, because I had a burning desire to play faster, better— and know it mattered to someone.

Looking at my grinning face in the photo made me sick. If I'd known what was in store for me, would I have said yes to his offer?

Rage filled me. Out of nowhere, it seared through my gut and exploded through my mouth. I got off the bench and tried to lift it up, straining with the effort, but it was bolted down. I kicked it, yelling curses at the top of my lungs. Then ran to the chain-link fence and slammed my body against it, clawing, trying to shake it loose.

I'd let him do things to me. I wailed at what I'd let happen. It was too much. To think about it squeezed my head, the thoughts ramming against my brain inside and out. I couldn't get free of them.

I was on the ground, racked by sobs. My gut sore, my mind wasted, my body rotting.

Something wet and warm on my fingers. Storm licking me. She nuzzled against my arm and lay down in the crook of my armpit.

Hope's poems sat in a ball a few feet away, white against the green grass.

She never knew about Coach Williams. No one did.

HOPE

A blackbird landed on the branch outside my window, its wing feathers spread like fingers. An ugly squawk when it opened its mouth.

I'd put off calling Mom for as long as I could, but the curiosity was killing me. Knowing would be better than wondering. Mom answered on the second ring, like she was waiting by the phone. Maybe she was.

"Have you heard from Eric?" she asked right away.

I closed my eyes with relief. If she was looking for him, he was still alive, the worst hadn't happened. "No. Why?"

A slight hesitation. "Oh, no reason. I just wondered if he'd checked in with you. He"—she dropped her voice. I imagined her going into the kitchen, escaping to somewhere Dad couldn't hear her—"hasn't been by in a few days."

That wasn't unusual for Eric. He'd probably crashed somewhere, exhausted after days of being awake. She took a long breath. It echoed in my ear, magnified by the phone. "Is there something else?" I asked. She sounded more concerned than normal. We'd gotten used to his sporadic appearances.

"No," she answered too quickly.

"Look, if you're really worried, leave him some food in the old tree stump. If it's gone, you'll know he's okay." I felt like a traitor for spilling our secret.

She gave a mirthless laugh. "The stump? Where you used to build forts? That's where you …" Her voice trailed off. *Looked after him*, the unspoken words. Gave him the help that his own mother wouldn't, or couldn't: clothes from his room, notes to tell him when Dad would be gone, leftovers disappeared from the fridge. "You never told me."

"I should have," I said, but didn't mean it. It wasn't her right to know everything about us.

We made small talk for a few minutes. She asked about school, how I was settling in, who I was spending my time with. I lied, making my time at Ravenhurst sound better than it was. I told her Cassie and I hung out, and I invented friendships with other girls. If she knew how unhappy I was, she'd suggest I come home and I didn't want to do that. At Ravenhurst, I could forget about Eric and pretend my fractured family was whole again.

Thursday, September 18, 11:45 p.m.
To: Hope
From: Devon
Subject: Hi from Hellton

It's after curfew. I'm not supposed to be on my computer, but I couldn't sleep. Are you staying at Ravenhurst this weekend? We

should meet up. What's your cell number?
Mine is 555-3009
D.

Friday, September 19, 8:04 a.m.
To: Devon
From: Hope
Subject: Weekend

There's a coffee shop on the corner of Harrow
and Garfield St. Do you know it? We could meet
there. 1:00 p.m. on Saturday? 555–7893
Hope

I hadn't known what to think about his emails at
first. No guy had ever approached me before, either in
real life or online. My replies had been cautious at first.
Who was he? He'd just seen my profile picture in the
online student directory and sent me a message? Wasn't
that kind of weird? But how else would he meet girls at
an all-boys school?

He'd been at Melton since he was twelve and hated
it. He knew some of the Ravens because our schools
did activities together. He thought they were bitchy and
stuck-up. That's why he liked me. I wasn't part of that
world. When I read that, I knew I could trust him.

I'd get to meet him tomorrow. My heart gave a leap
of excitement, followed quickly by nasty voices in my
head. What if he didn't like me? What if the relationship
we'd created online was stilted and uncomfortable when
we met face to face?

I pushed the negativity out of my head. Maybe he
was the soulmate friend I'd been looking for. I'd always

thought it would be a girl, but why? Devon was so much easier to talk to. There wasn't any drama or hidden meanings that I didn't know how to decode.

I started to send a message to Devon and glimpsed the remains of the poem I'd scrawled on myself days ago. Like almost-erased footprints, I followed the track backwards to my elbow. I'd scrub it off tonight in the shower. The last thing I wanted was for Devon to see my insecurities laid bare on my flesh.

ERIC

All I could think about was getting high. Each footstep was one closer to a fix. My body pulsed with the thought of it. I tried the rubbing alcohol I'd stolen from the pharmacy, soaking my shirt with it and sniffing it, but it just gave me a headache and burned my nose. No good.

I'd made it into the city—past the winding butterfly highway, through an industrial area that stunk with belching factories—and found a park. There were places to hide, thickets of trees I could camp in, and washrooms. Luxury not to have to squat and wipe my ass with leaves. But nothing helped the greyness that suffocated me without meth.

Not the bottle of whiskey I'd found hidden in the bushes, sucking back the few drops of amber liquid at the bottom. Or the submarine sandwich some girl had handed me out of her car window. Everything was dull. A flat line.

Storm wanted to run. She tugged on the leash. The gauze was dirty, bits of grass and sand had gotten tangled in the fabric. We'd spent the last two nights in the park, hiding from the park police who patrolled. It was getting colder at night. I'd hugged Storm against me, shivering in my jacket and unable to sleep.

Storm strained at the gauze, her front paws pedalling in mid-air. "What is it?" I asked, annoyed. Standing up, I let her lead me but had to run to keep up with her. Her breath came in jagged gasps in her determination to get somewhere.

She led me to a clump of bushes, where a dog, still on its leash, was tangled up inside. I rubbed Storm's head and crawled in. The dog barked at me. "Don't be scared," I said softly. He tried to move backwards into the bush, away from me, but the branches wouldn't let him. I kept talking as I untangled his leash, finally pulling him out. Burrs and leaves were all over his coat and I wondered how long he'd been trapped in there.

The new dog had a silver tag in the shape of a heart: LOUIE and a phone number.

It took some convincing to get the park office to let me use their phone. The woman at the front desk shot me a horrified look when I walked in. Without the smells and noises of outside, I was exposed. Conspicuous inside an office with carpet and furniture, I itched to get back outside.

"It's just to call the owner," I told her, trying to control my temper. "I found her dog." The woman didn't know what to do and called security.

"If I had any change, I'd use a pay phone," I mumbled. "But I don't." The security guy stood over me as I dialled, two dogs at my feet sniffing each other's butts.

HOPE

Why hadn't he shown up? I'd sat in the café for half an hour, breathing in the smell of freshly baked scones and percolating coffee and flipping the pages of a book without reading a word. I'd chosen the book carefully, something that would impress him. Hoping I looked brainy but not pretentious. As I sat at a table by the window, I forced my eyes to stare at the pages, not the door. My phone sat in front of me, frustratingly silent. I'd turned it on and off twice to ensure it was in good working order. Where was he?

Lizzie, Emily, and Vivian walked past outside, their arms linked so they took up the whole sidewalk. I slouched down in my chair. It was the third time I'd seen them go past. This time, Lizzie paused at the glass. The gold letters spelling out "Grace's Café" on the window were at eye level, obscuring her vision. She sank down, our faces inches apart but separated by glass. I felt like a zoo animal as she peered at me, her breath fogging the window.

Turning to my book, I tried to concentrate, but she kept staring. My heart beat faster and I angled my chair away from the window, reaching for my glass of water. I glanced at the clock. Devon was now forty minutes late. Why? Was he sick? Had he forgotten? Had he seen the Ravens mocking me at the window and turned away? A list of reasons for him not showing ran through my head, and a sick feeling rose in my stomach.

I should text him. What if something was wrong? But—and the thought made my heart ache—what if he *had* come and then chosen to leave? Texting him and not getting a reply would confirm it.

"Love." The owner, a short woman with reddish hair and a ruddy complexion, waddled to my table. "Are you going to order something? Can't have you sitting here all day with only a glass of water."

I glanced out the window. The Ravens had disappeared from view. "Sorry. I was waiting for someone, but I guess they aren't coming." I shut the book, not bothering to turn down the page. Just then, a tall, good-looking boy came in. His hair was brown, like Devon's. It could be him! A rising wave of hope flooded through me and I looked at him with an expectant smile, waiting for him to spot me.

He did. His eyes flickered over me and then to the table behind me, where an older couple sat. They rose to give him a welcoming hug. It wasn't Devon. My face fell and the owner clamped a hand onto my shoulder.

"I've some day-olds in the back," she said. "Did you want one to take with you?"

She was kind, but pastries weren't going to lift the heavy weight of disappointment that had settled in my stomach. He hadn't come. Or had, but then changed his mind about meeting me.

She bustled back in a moment with a white paper bag. Butter had already leaked through, dotting it with shiny grey spots.

"Thanks," I muttered, fumbling with my jacket, and darted toward the door. The old brass doorknob turned in my hand and I slid outside. The air had turned chilly overnight. Leaves from the old oak trees overhead floated down. When I shut the door, all three Ravens were in front of me. Standing a few inches too close, I had no choice but to look at them.

Lizzie smiled, her eyes narrowed to slits. "Waiting for someone?"

"No," I answered quickly.

"Really? It looked like you were. I wonder why he didn't come? I assume it was a boy. You fixed your hair. It almost looks nice." She hissed the last word.

I gritted my teeth and turned in the other direction, but all three shuffled in front of me. I was trapped.

The café door jingled open. "Your bag, love! You left it on the chair." The owner stood halfway outside, my purse extended at the end of her mottled, fleshy arm. Lizzie and her friends moved aside so I could take it. "What are you three up to? Seen you standing out here loitering. Get on with you before I call the school. You know the rules. Go on!" She shooed them away with a flap of her hand.

They shot me a warning glance and turned away, hair shining in the sun, and linked arms again, like carefree schoolgirls.

"Best stay away from those ones." She gave me a look of motherly concern and went back inside.

I wished I could.

ERIC

Louie's owner gave me $200 as a reward.

But it was tainted. The way she'd handed it to me, like I didn't deserve it, even though she'd told me on the phone that if it was Louie I'd found, she'd pay.

I tried to tell her where I'd found him, but she was in such a rush to get away from me that she didn't want to hear. Stuck-up bitch. *I'm as good as you*, I wanted to tell her. *You think you're so much better than me? Well, you're not.*

I didn't realize I was mumbling till a kid on a bike asked his dad who I was talking to.

Two-goddamned-hundred-fucking dollars! The thought coursed through my head. Finally, something good had happened. I had to be smart about this, I told Storm. Not blow it all at once. I had to find a place to crash first, and warm clothes. And a leash for Storm, so she wouldn't get lost.

And then, the sweet hereafter. I'd find a dealer.

The money was all in twenties, fresh from a bank machine. The wad of cash bulged in my back pocket. I put it in the one with a button so it wouldn't fall out. Safe with Hope's poems.

Ha! Hope. I didn't need to find her now. If I did, I could show her how well I was doing on my own.

Some kids sat on a grassy field, playing guitars and a bongo. Hippies. From the walking path, I could smell the pot they weren't being very careful to hide. "Hey, man!" I called and raised a hand in greeting. Storm tugged at the leash to get closer to them, desperate to be friends with everyone. "You guys know anyone around here?" I asked, waiting to see if my vague question would be understood.

"What are looking for?" a guy with shaggy blond hair asked, eyeing me.

I crouched down so we were all at the same level. "Crank, if you got any."

A shadow of distaste crossed his face. "Nah, man, we don't do that shit. You gotta head downtown for that."

There was a girl with them. She wasn't pretty—her nose was too big and she had huge, buggy eyes—but I used to be able to get what I wanted from girls. "Well, what do you guys have?" I asked her.

She took me in and pulled her legs under her skirt self-consciously. "Just the pot."

"You mind, man?" The blond guy said. "This is a private party."

I stood up and yanked on Storm's leash, pulling her away from sniffing their blanket, on the hunt for some food. "I don't mind," I said, sneering at them. As if I wanted to hang out with a bunch of hippies anyway. "Which way's downtown?" I called to them as I walked away.

They pointed to a bridge that crossed a river.

I didn't have time to wait for Storm to pee. I hurried her along, half dragging her toward whatever lay downtown, at the promised land of dark alleys and vacant buildings.

HOPE

I couldn't concentrate on my homework. Words floated around me like a mist. I grabbed some of them, lifting up the hem of my skirt and inscribing them on my thigh, vandalizing my body.

> Thick shadows
> Suffocate
> Pressing from all sides,
> Gasping, I struggle.
> Like a noose
> They get tighter.

There hadn't been any emails or texts from Devon. No explanation about why he hadn't shown up. I'd spent the rest of the weekend moping, going over in my mind every possible reason he hadn't shown. Some of them gave me hope, and others turned dark and twisted.

The mattress springs squeaked. I felt along the wooden frame under my quilt. I'd carved a poem into it last night. I liked the feel of the gouged letters, under my fingertips.

I had a history mid-term to study for. But every time I opened a book the words swam across the page and my mind started to wander. Even in class, I zoned out. Sometimes it was about the Ravens, what-if questions: *What if I'd cut Cassie's hair? What if I'd never started hanging out with them? What if I'd never left Lumsville?* But always my thoughts drifted back to Devon: *What if he'd shown up?* A vicious circle.

There was a beep from my computer. I had a message. Scrambling to my desk, I opened my email, praying that it was from Devon.

> Monday, September 22, 4:04 p.m.
> **To:** Hope
> **From:** Devon
> **Subject:** Sorry
>
> Sorry I didn't meet you in town. I've been sick. Food poisoning or something. I really wanted to meet you, and I'm not just saying that. Let's try again on Saturday. I promise not to eat the cafeteria's Friday Night Surprise again.
> D.

I laughed out loud with relief when I read Devon's email. He'd had food poisoning. Oh, thank God! I'd never been so happy to hear someone was sick in my life. He hadn't stood me up. The knot of worry in my stomach unravelled and turned to feathers, tickling my insides.

I couldn't wipe the smile off my face as I replied to his email.

finding hope

Monday, September 22, 4:08 p.m.
To: Devon
From: Hope
Subject: Weekend

I hope you're feeling better! I was so sad when
you didn't show up.
    I'd love to meet you this weekend, but
it's actually my birthday, so my mom is either
coming in to the city, or I'm going home this
weekend. ☹ At least it means a break from RH,
but it screws up our plans to get together.
H.

Tuesday, September 23, 6:32 p.m.
To: Hope
From: Devon
Re: Weekend

I want to celebrate your birthday. We should go
out somewhere for dinner, but it can't be the
weekend after next, because that's homecoming
and my parents are coming in. We'll discuss
their favourite topic: whether or not I have a
girlfriend. Wish I knew what to say ...
D.

Tuesday, September 23, 6:35 p.m.
To: Devon
From: Hope
Subject: !!!!

What's that supposed to mean?! Email back
right away and EXPLAIN YOURSELF! If you're
asking what I think you're asking, then YES!
Love, H.

ERIC

The streets got dirtier. A few abandoned buildings with plywood nailed over their windows, weeds growing up the sides of the houses, and empty lots filled with garbage. It smelled gritty here, like gravel and exhaust. A steady stream of cars flowed past, pressing forward.

Storm and I hurried too. She was giddy like me, leaping, then catching the leash in her mouth and trying to play with it. The wad of cash thick in my pocket. I'd get mugged if I didn't spend it.

A beige car drove past. Mom's car. The brake lights flashed on, glowing candy-apple red and my throat squeezed shut. She'd come to find me. The elation I felt shocked me.

But when I looked again, I saw that the woman in this car had long blonde hair. It didn't stick out frizzy like mom's. And she was tall. Mom's head didn't go past the back of the seat. I stared at her through the window. She looked straight ahead, maybe ignoring me. Or maybe just not seeing me.

I wondered if Mom had noticed I'd left Lumsville, or if she even cared?

"What are you doing?" Like a keening animal, she'd asked that question too many times. When I came home hyped on meth, when I raged in my room for no reason that she understood, when I ran my bank account dry, when I sold my hockey gear, when I punched Dick, when I stole her bank card.

I never answered her. Not with the truth, anyway.

"What are you doing, Mom?" I should have fired back. Letting me go off with a hockey coach we barely knew, letting him drive me and stay in hotels with me, letting him touch me and making me touch him. *What were you doing, Mom, to let that happen?*

Hot anger pulsed through me. My hands clenched, balling up into fists at my sides. Black seeped into the corner of my eyes, making everything go dark.

A guy, one who looked like me, only with a full beard and wearing a baseball cap, crossed the street and bent down to pat Storm. I yanked her away from him, too hard. She slipped and yelped.

He stood up and watched me, small blue eyes peeking out from a grizzled face. Coach Williams had blue eyes. "What the fuck are you looking at?" I said. Yelled. He stepped away and held up his hands in surrender.

I took a step closer to him, intimidating. He backed up until he was against a wall. Broken shards of stucco lay at his feet.

"Don't you follow me! Leave me alone!" I screamed in his face.

He shrank from me, protecting his face. Emblazoned on his inner arm was a tattoo of a cross, with points like a dagger. A dagger through the heart. It pierced me.

I could feel it go in and slide out, thick, oozing blood dripping from it.

But it wasn't my blood. The guy's nose was bleeding. Had I done that? I stared at the throbbing knuckles on my right hand. He cowered against the wall, begging me to leave him alone. Storm barked, warning me of something.

"Run!" her bark said. So we did.

HOPE

A package wrapped in silver paper appeared outside my door before dinner. A big red ribbon was tied around it and a gift tag dangled from the bow:

> For Hope
> Have a happy birthday, even if it's with-
> out me.
> Love, Devon

I stared at the box, a warm, gooey feeling melting my insides. I marvelled at how Devon was able to surprise me, to make me feel so special. I never knew what to expect from him. Had he brought it to RH himself? Or mailed it?

Stroking the satin bow, I pulled one end of the ribbon until it pooled on my bed, the red clashing against the pastel colours of the quilt. I ripped the paper off the box and pulled out a teddy bear, honey brown with shiny black eyes. A silver necklace glinted around his neck. My face broke into a smile as I held the pendant dangling from it in my hand and noticed the engraving: LOVE, DEVON.

I pressed the bear to my chest, taking a joyful inhalation of his synthetic fur, revelling in Devon's attentions.

Propping the bear up on my pillow, I went to the mirror and fiddled with the clasp of the necklace. The heart hung past my collarbones, slightly obscured by my blouse. I didn't care if other people could see it, as long as I could feel the cool weight of it against my skin.

ERIC

I kept looking behind me to see if the guy with the bleeding nose had followed us, but he hadn't. I yanked on Storm's leash and dragged her with me into an alley, sinking down against a brick wall. Storm licked my face, jumping up and down from all the excitement.

From across the street, some guy kept yelling "Hey, Calvin!" until I turned. He was older than me, or maybe he wasn't. Meth fucks up your face. He was skinny, knobby elbows and bony shoulders sticking out of his T-shirt. He ambled over, a breeze blowing his hair—one side shaved, the other long and stringy—across his face.

"Where you been, man?" he asked and held out his hand. "God, it's been fucking forever since you been back here."

I looked at him funny. Never seen him before in my life, I was sure of it. But if he could hook me up, I'd be whoever the hell he wanted me to be.

We were on a street where I knew I'd be able to score. People milled around, pushing shopping carts, stumbling. A couple of kids with dirty faces stared at me from a second-storey window. Pavement everywhere, not one bit of green, except for some weeds growing between sidewalk cracks. The air smelled dank, like rotting garbage, but there weren't many cars around here. Only a few, going real slow. Maybe looking for a dealer or a hooker. There were a few girls, hanging around on corners and stoops. Nasty-looking.

"I'm looking to party. You know anyone?" I asked. Storm had found a newspaper and was quietly shredding it at my feet.

He looked at me like I was crazy. Which was kind of funny, since he was the one calling me Calvin.

"Who do you think you're talking to? Goddamned smartass! Course I can hook you up! Jesus fucking Christ, how long you been gone?" He gave me a wide smile. Brown, rotting teeth filled his mouth. He'd been on meth for a long time. "You got a place to stay?"

I shook my head.

"You do now," he said and nodded with his head that I should follow him. He walked on his toes, like an invisible balloon was tugging at him. "The place hasn't changed much. Brandi is still here. Had a kid, but it got taken away. I never saw the other guy you were hanging with after you left." He led me across the street to a house with a boarded-up front window. Graffiti covered the door, and the lock was broken.

Holes had been punched in the walls and there was more writing on them, like insane, scribbled thoughts. A few random pieces of furniture in each room, mattresses, old wooden chairs, a card table, a lamp with no shade. Some of the windows had sheets for curtains, or cardboard.

"Look who I found!" the guy crowed when we got to the kitchen. A girl, her mouth slack and eyes glazed over, didn't move. The kitchen faucet dripped. Opened boxes of food and used plates sat on a chipped white countertop. An indistinct rancid smell got worse when the guy opened the fridge.

"Remember Calvin?" he asked her. She didn't respond. Storm sniffed around the corners and lunged for a mouse that skittered across the floor and shot behind the fridge.

"I got money," I told him. "How about twenty bucks' worth, and maybe a place to chill for a while?" My foot tapped impatiently. I had the cash, I just wanted the stuff. Warning bells were ringing, though. This wasn't Lumsville. No one here knew me. No one was looking out for me.

"Yeah, anything for you, man. You get clean or what? Twenty bucks didn't used to last you a couple hours before you left." He laughed.

Shrugging, I pulled a bill out from my pocket, careful to hide what was left. Twenty dollars would last me a day, maybe more. Once I had some juice running through me, I could plan what to do next. My brain couldn't function without it anymore.

"You wanna do a line with me?" he asked.

I could taste it, my teeth already grinding in anticipation. I wanted the hit so bad now that it was so close.

I followed him upstairs. LEO was scrawled across the door in black marker. "Hey, Leo," I said, checking that that was his name.

He turned and gave me a toothless smile.

"Glad to be back."

HOPE

The handles on the plastic shopping bags twisted around my fingers, leaving deep grooves when I deposited them onto the floor under our table. We'd made it to a restaurant after spending the afternoon at the mall.

I hadn't told Mom about Devon. Not yet. The necklace he'd sent was tucked into my pocket, waiting to be revealed. I wanted her to be excited for me. He was my first official boyfriend. Smart and funny, he knew just what to say to make me feel better.

It would matter to Mom that I'd never met him. I'd have to explain that I felt like I *knew* him better than I knew anyone else.

I deserved to have someone like Devon in my life. For so long, everything had revolved around Eric. First, his hockey games, his future, and when he'd quit that, the drugs had taken over. We were always talking about his problems, his needs. I never knew how much it bothered me until I had some of my own. Until I was bursting to share my own news.

I took the pendant out of my pocket, letting it drape across my leg. The silver heart caught the light, glinting under the table. Smiling, I said, "Mom, I have to tell you something." She wasn't listening.

"Mom?" I tried again.

Her forehead creased with worry. Our annual mother–daughter shopping trip was in honour of my birthday, but now that we were sitting down, without the chaos of a mall to absorb me, I could see how distracted she was. "There's something I need to tell you." I clutched the necklace, fingering the chain.

"The police are looking for Eric," she blurted. Her mouth drew into a tight line. Lipstick had bled up into the feathery wrinkles around her lips.

I let the necklace go and rubbed my forehead. Even here, at my birthday dinner, with news of my boyfriend burning a hole in my throat, Eric had taken over. "Why? What did he do?"

"Broke into the pharmacy. Two weeks ago."

"What?" I shook my head in confusion. "Two weeks ago? Where'd he go?"

Tears filled her eyes when she looked at me. "I don't know," she whispered.

We sat at the table, silent. The server refilled our water glasses and then quickly left. Ice cubes clinked, like grinding teeth, making space for themselves.

"Did you leave something in the stump, like I said?"

She nodded. "It was still there this morning."

I took a deep, shaky breath. My brother was out there somewhere. If he was high, he wasn't eating or sleeping. If he wasn't high, he was doing anything he had to in order to get high. "I thought maybe he'd called you. Let you know where he was, or something."

Her voice trailed off and she used a napkin to wipe her eyes.

I thought about lying and saying he had, to make the pained look on her face disappear, but then what? My brother was missing and there was nothing I could do.

I looked away and fingered the prongs of my fork, letting each one press into the flesh of my finger.

I stuffed the pendant back into my pocket.

ERIC

I could concentrate now that the crank was running through me. I had so much to do. There were plans to make. Places I had to go. I needed to get things. I had to see Hope. Let her know I was okay. She'd tell Mom, not that Mom gave a shit. She and Dick probably didn't even notice I wasn't in Lumsville anymore.

I was being a shit. They'd notice. Mom would worry. But a voice in my head said, *Not true.* They'd let me go with that fucking pervert. Thank God I had meth. It helped me deal with everything. Meth helped me get through the dark nights—not Mom or Dick. Who gave a fuck if they were hurting? It would never be as much as I was.

But that didn't matter right now, I reminded myself and tried to stay focused. My mind raced. I had a lot to do. I'd gone through a dresser in Calvin's room and found an old notebook, the kind kids use at school, and a pencil. I stuffed everything into my pocket, moving the poems and cash to a zippered pocket on the inside of my jacket. Wasn't as thick as it used to be, that wad of cash.

But that didn't matter. Nothing mattered. I had what mattered; it was in me. Coursing through me like race cars on a speedway track.

Oh, I was feeling good. Better. Best.

Leo still called me Calvin, but I didn't care. It was better if Eric was gone, left behind on that long stretch of highway between Lumsville and the city. I liked talking to Leo. He listened to me. I told him all about my hockey, how good I was, how far I almost went. He asked what happened. I told him. Coach Williams.

The name stuck. It kept sticking, like a cog in a machine that wouldn't move. Or a scratched CD. I couldn't get past Coach Williams.

What happened to him? Leo wanted to know.

I told him. Moved to the city.

Moved to the city.

And then that got stuck in my head. Stabbing into my brain, like a shard of glass.

Coach Williams was in the city.

HOPE

My phone beeped with a text.

> Do you really care about me? Or are you just
> saying you do to keep me around?
> D.

My stomach dropped when I read it. It wasn't the first time I'd seen his insecure side. Devon worried about all kinds of ridiculous things: that I was cheating on him, that I didn't really like him, that I was laughing at him; things that couldn't be further from the truth. I knew how to handle it though: I'd send a message reassuring him that I cared more about him than anyone else.

A day would pass and he'd send me an apologetic text, blaming his mood on Melton and how much he hated it there. He'd thank me for being understanding, and say that without me, he had nothing.

I hadn't told Devon that my brother was missing. I didn't like keeping a secret from him, but our relationship was the one thing in my life that hadn't been tainted by Eric and his problems. As soon as I told Devon the ugly, sordid truth, it would be.

Devon had asked once why I'd chosen Ravenhurst. I'd told him it wasn't because of the friendliness of students (LOL!), but that I'd wanted to get out of Lumsville. If I'd been honest, I would have told him about Eric right then. That as much as I loved my brother, he was tearing me apart. And that I didn't want to be Eric Randall's little sister anymore, I just wanted to be me, to have an identity that wasn't linked to Eric the Hockey Player, or Eric the Junkie.

So, when he sent me a text, questioning our relationship, all my energy went to reassuring him. Making sure he knew how much he meant to me. I couldn't lose him now.

> Friday, October 3, 9:44 p.m.
> **From:** Hope
>
> Whenever this place gets to be too much, I touch my necklace and everything feels better. It's like you're with me all the time. You are the only thing making this place bearable.
>
> Dangling
> From a thread
> Suspended, breath
> Catching in my throat.
> The drop won't kill me.
> But how will I catch
> What I lost?

Friday, October 3, 9:50 p.m.
From: Devon

We should run away together. Where would we
go? Anywhere is good. As long as it's me and
you …

His words made me melt. I read each text over and
over wishing he was beside me, to hear the words from
his own lips. Some days, I wanted to talk to him so badly.
To know that I wasn't alone.

Mom called me daily with reports. No one had
heard from Eric and the police had turned up nothing.
Mom and I had run over the possibilities. He must have
come to the city. Where else would he go? But he had
no money. He could have hitch-hiked, we reasoned, and
was probably holed up in the city, but where? I scanned
the gates of the school, huge metal ones with an auto
sensor and an alarm on them. I was sure that one day
he'd show up outside of them, begging to be let in.

The other possibility, the one that neither Mom or I
said out loud, was that he was dead. We both knew the
lifespan of a meth addict was five years. We'd done our
research at the beginning of his addiction. "You're going
to die!" we'd told him. But he didn't care.

That's when I knew the meth had him. Nothing we
could do would loosen its hold.

I flipped through my journal. And found an empty
page.

Serrated tentacles strangle
The life out of you.

Whipping across your future,
Cutting it to shreds,
Inescapable.
We struggle for you.
But we get sliced
Out of your life.

"Fuck you, Eric," I whispered.

Tears fell onto the paper, splotches of wetness that blurred the lines. Nothing was clear anymore.

ERIC

Storm pressed her nose against my cheek. I pushed her away, but she nipped at my finger, like we were playing a game.

Burying my head under the pillow, I tried to ignore the hunger pains rumbling through my stomach. I needed to sleep.

The smell of shit made me open my eyes. She'd taken a dump on the floor in front of me. "Fuck, Storm!" I shouted. She bolted to the other side of the room and hung her head. Her tail stopped wagging.

I looked around. What difference did it make in this hole? A pile of steaming dog shit was an improvement.

How long had I been out? And, before that, how long had we been amped? I didn't know what day it was or even if it was still September. Days, weeks, months blurred, they swam past me. The world lost focus.

Cramps ripped through my insides. I needed to eat. I reached into my pocket. Thin. Where had the wad gone? I'd been robbed. Mugged by one of the assholes in the house. Fucking junkies.

Rage boiled in me. I pulled everything out of my pockets. The rubbing alcohol was gone too. No, it wasn't. It was on the floor beside my mattress. Hope's poems, the photos—I let everything fall to the floor.

They'd left me with one fucking twenty-dollar bill. Had it been Leo, parading around as my friend, doling out his lines to me?

I went looking for the bastard, stumbling down the hallway. I opened the door with his name on it, but his mattress was empty.

As I walked down the creaky steps, I had a flash of memory. I'd given him some of the money. In an act of speed-induced generosity. How much? I'd stuffed some bills into his sweaty hand, insisting he take them. "You're the best, Calvin," he'd said.

I had to sit down on the stairs as the memory sank in. Storm nosed me. Absently, I patted her head. I could feel her heart beating fast in her chest. "Come on, Storm," I said and stood up, hanging on to the banister so I didn't tumble down the stairs.

The kitchen was empty. Every cupboard, bare. A cloudy glass sat in the sink. I filled it and drank till I thought my stomach would burst. The water tasted metallic, slimy on my tongue.

I was going to pass out if I didn't get something to eat. On the table, an old loaf of bread. I ripped the plastic bag open and stuffed a piece into my mouth. Under the bread was my notebook, the one with CALVIN scrawled on the front. My writing—messy, barely legible—filled the pages.

I leafed through it, trying to make sense of the words. There were lists, plans, things I needed to do.

Everything urgent. Filled with exclamation marks and underlined.

One whole page with nothing but Coach Williams' name written on it.

I rushed to the sink, barely making it before I vomited up the bread and water. Undigested. It gushed out, filling the sink.

HOPE

I knew he'd come.

When Ms. Harrison knocked on my door at eight o'clock at night and asked me to come with her, I didn't ask why. I followed the staccato clip of her sensible heels through the common room. The urgency of her steps drew the attention of the other girls. I kept my head down, ignoring their curious looks. The echo of her footsteps stopped when we got to the cavernous front entrance. We were alone, except for the security guard who sat at his desk, surrounded by monitors.

"I don't want to upset you," she warned me. "But someone at the front gates wants to see you. He claims to be your brother, Eric."

I let out a sigh of relief. He was alive.

And at the gates of my school.

My stomach twisted. The reprieve was over.

Ms. Harrison put a hand on my shoulder and met my eyes. She could have been pretty in a willowy way. Thin lips, pointed nose, a body like a ballerina's, but she went out of her way to dress like a spinster. In her long skirts and prim blouses, I could almost see cats winding themselves around her ankles as she sipped tea. "You don't have to see him, if you don't want to. We can tell him to leave." I could see the concern in her face. "We could call your parents."

"No," I said quickly, "they told me he might come by."

She looked at me doubtfully. "It's unusual for a sibling to show up at our school like this, Hope." Her meaning was clear. The security guard would have tipped her off. He'd been on his own for almost three weeks.

"He's always like this, really unpredictable," I reassured her. "But he's not dangerous or anything."

She hesitated. Panic seized me at the possibility of not being allowed to see him, but I stayed mute, giving her my best impression of wide-eyed innocence. Ms. Harrison sighed and relented. She ushered me to the security guard's station so he could point to a blurry figure on the security monitor, pacing in front of the gates.

My voice caught in my throat. It was him. I looked at Ms. Harrison. "That's Eric," I said.

She nodded for the security guard to buzz the front doors open. Suddenly desperate to see him, to know he was okay, I raced across the parking lot.

"Eric!" I shouted when I was within arm's length of the gates. Scrolled black iron, they cast dramatic shadows under the amber street lights.

He turned. I recoiled.

His face was skeletal—sunken cheeks, hollowed eyes. His hair lay matted and twisted on his head, unwashed. And his clothes. I shuddered at the filth. He had the jacket, the one I'd left for him. Why did that make me feel better? He still looked like death. The jacket probably weighed as much as he did. His body odour made my eyes water. He must have been wearing those clothes since he left Lumsville.

"Haha!" he laughed, holding onto the bars and jumping up and down. As if he'd won a million dollars. "I told the fucker you went here! See!" He pointed at the security guard. "You see! I told you she was my sister." Triumphant.

And then he started rambling. About someone named Storm, who he'd left at home. And about Calvin, and how he'd found a place to crash but needed money. He wouldn't have bothered me if it wasn't important. He just really, really needed some cash. He'd pay me back, he promised.

Tears welled in my eyes as he spoke. He was high, amped up on the meth. His movements continuous, one long, jerky circle as he hopped, paced, and twitched. I curled my toes, willing him to stop. Slow down. Be my brother.

Mom had warned me not to help him if I saw him. To call her and she'd deal with it. But watching him in front of me, I felt myself crumble. He'd come to find me. Of everyone, I was the person he counted on. I couldn't let him down.

"Eric." I just wanted him to look at me. To stop moving for one minute so I could see his face, find some glimmer of the person I used to know. "Eric!" I said louder, trying to get his attention.

He stopped, his eyes wide, grinning at me. Like a cartoon, a funhouse creation at a carnival. "Here, take this," he said and passed a scribbler to me through the bars.

"Everything's in there. All my plans. Read it, okay? It's really important." And then he gripped the bars, pressing his face against them, urgent and intense. "Don't lose it, Hope. We'll need it."

We.

"Why? What's the plan?" I asked, playing along.

He gave me a sweet smile and my heart melted. "You'll see. Just read it, okay? I'll come back soon." He started to walk away and then turned back. "Oh, shit. Hope," he said, jamming his hands into his pockets, then pulling them out again, running them through his hair, over his face, rubbing his neck, sticking them back into his pockets. "Got any cash on you? Like, anything at all? I swear, I'll pay you back."

My breath came quick, a heat rising up in my stomach. Mom had said not to. But what would he do if I didn't?

"Come back tomorrow," I told him in a rush, before I lost my nerve.

Eric sneered. "I need it now. Fuck."

He needed it now to get high. By tomorrow, he'd have crashed and he'd be looking to eat. I knew the pattern.

"I don't have any now," I told him firmly. Like how Mom would set rules, just before she broke them.

He seethed at me and I was glad there were bars between us. It wasn't him, though. It was the meth, coursing through his blood, making a devil appear where my brother used to be.

ERIC

When I woke up, it was daytime. Light filtered through the dirty window in Calvin's room. I needed to shower. I couldn't go back to Hope's school looking like this. My skin crawled, ants streaming in a line from the top of my head to my toes, their little footsteps on every blood vessel. It wasn't blood in my veins, but ants. Digging a fingernail into my flesh, I tested the theory. Red blood surged up.

Okay, no ants. But still, the feeling. I groaned. A shower would wash the filth off. Leo told me about a place not too far away. Food, showers. Some kind of shelter. You had to talk to someone first, before they let you in. But it would be worth it, to feel human for a while.

I'd given Hope my scribbler. I wish I hadn't, but it was probably safer with her anyway. I'd almost burned it a while back. Somehow, it made sense to light it on fire and watch it go up in flames. I couldn't find a lighter, though. So I hadn't burned it.

Storm was sleeping in the corner. I'd found a box for her and lined it with some old clothes I found in Calvin's closet. She liked it, snuffled around in circles until she got comfortable. I'd leave her here in case they didn't let dogs into this place.

The school had looked like a fortress, all gloomy with gates like a prison. I couldn't imagine my little sister locked up in there. Did she like it? I wish I'd asked. I didn't remember what we had talked about, if she was happy to see me or not.

A pang of regret hit me in the gut. I missed her. At home we were on the same team; we had each other's backs. Not now though. She was stuck behind the gates and I was on the outside.

I'd go back tonight. Had I told her tonight, or last night? The days blurred together. Maybe she'd been waiting for me to show, a few bills rolled tightly in her fist, while I'd been here, sleeping. My head ached trying to figure it out. I'd stay sober until after I saw her, I promised myself.

See Hope. Take a hit. I balled my fists up in a silent pledge.

The sun seared my eyeballs when I stepped outside. After spending so long in the dark, I had to stand still for a minute to let my pupils adjust.

I didn't know how long I'd been in the city, but the air was cold. I zipped up the jacket, and the leather collar rubbed against my ears. It still smelled like leather, musky, but the stink of the house had found its way into the skin as well. Something sour, dead.

I missed having Storm with me, straining on the end of her leash as I walked to the shelter. I got nervous being by myself. Kept turning around to see if anyone was following me.

There was a line of people, all the same dingy colour as me, stretched around a brick building, waiting for the doors of the shelter to open. Some of them mumbled to themselves, other looked like they were going to fall down from exhaustion, their faces shrivelled.

I got in line.

Seeing the other people, knowing I was the same as them, begging for handouts, reduced to this, made bile rise in my throat. I was supposed to be playing on a farm team this year, one step away from making it to the NHL. How had I ended up here? I looked around me in confusion. Was it a joke, this life? A cruel prank meant to teach me a lesson?

A hammering started in my head. I squeezed my eyes shut and my hands flew to my scalp, pulling at my hair, the strands clumped and greasy. A physical ache like I was being twisted in two.

It was wrong, all of it. I wasn't supposed to end up like this.

I went to the ground, holding my head and rocking. The line moved and people shuffled past. There was a guy staring at me. He had on a track jacket, black with red piping. AAA ALL-STARS. I remembered that jacket. Fuck, that jacket. A stream of obscenities lit from my mouth.

Coach Williams. He was everywhere. Hounding me. Wanting to take more, leave me empty, sucking me dry.

"Leave me alone!" I shouted. My face pulsed with anger.

I looked up again, but it wasn't Coach. This guy was old, his skin leathery. It wasn't even Coach's jacket. What the fuck was wrong with my eyes? He backed away from me. Everyone did.

The line started moving. They'd opened the doors.

It took me a minute to remember why I was here. A shower. Food.

Pushing myself up from the pavement, I shuffled inside, leaving what was left of me on the sidewalk.

HOPE

The notebook was nothing but gibberish. I wouldn't even have believed it was his. *Calvin* was written on the cover, but it was Eric's printing inside. I read it and reread it, trying to make sense out of what it meant. There were lists of things to do, things to buy, but most of it was nonsense.

He'd written pages of random words repeated over and over. *Coach Williams* took up three pages. And *Burn*. And then more pages of *x*, the pencil lead pressed so hard the page curled.

There was a blank sheet at the back. I used it to write a poem for him. I didn't know if he'd read it. I didn't know if he'd even come back, or if I wanted him to.

I groaned. Of course, I wanted him to. I just didn't want him consuming me.

> You
> On the other side
> Separated by bars
> From me.
> You think you're free

To come and go
Hell and back
Up and down.
Me, protected by the bars
From you.

I stuffed the scribbler under my mattress with twenty dollars of the birthday money Grandma had sent me. I cringed at what a sucker I was.

I'd held my cell in my hand twice, ready to call Mom. Almost dialling her number, and then tossing the phone onto my bed. If she knew he was in the city, that I'd seen him, she'd tell the cops. They'd take him away. He'd go to jail.

The weight of the secret was growing heavy. If he came back, I'd tell him Mom wanted to talk to him. That he should call her so she knew he was all right. I'd tell him she was worried about him. He might not care.

I pulled out the notebook and took out the twenty dollars. *Fuck you, Eric. Why should I help you?*

And then I felt like an asshole. Guilt hammered at me. It was only twenty bucks. He could get food. Or I could get food for him.

I nodded to myself with a sigh of relief. My stomach stopped churning. I'd give him money, but only if we spent it together and I got to see where he was living.

Cassie came into the room and I stuffed the notebook under my pillow, feeling ridiculous, like I had something to hide. She eyed me suspiciously. "Is it true?"

"Is what true?" I asked. Cassie still harboured distrust for what I may or may not have said about her; she kept her distance from me. I'd gotten tired of pleading innocence with her, and had given up completely on ever being friends with the Ravens. Which was just as well, since they acted like I no longer existed.

"Some of the girls saw you talking to a guy yesterday at the gates."

I froze. My jaw clenched.

"Do you have a boyfriend?"

"It's not what they think," I mumbled.

She looked at me, one eyebrow raised skeptically. Her face softened. "You can tell me, you know. I can keep a secret."

I shook my head. "Seriously, that wasn't my boy-friend."

Her mouth twisted into a scowl. "Who else would show up for you at eight o'clock on a Friday night?"

"Fine," I said with an exasperated sigh. "Yes, that was my boyfriend." If Eric showed up again, it would be easier to pass him off as my boyfriend than as who he really was. The only ones who might guess the truth were the Ravens.

"Did he send you that?" She pointed to the teddy bear on my bed.

I nodded. We settled into a comfortable silence and I took a deep breath. "Cassie, I really didn't say anything to Lizzie about you."

Our eyes met. It was exhausting being mad at some-one, especially a roommate.

"This is what they do, you know. Turn people against each other. It's, like, their hobby." She flopped down onto her bed, feet planted on the floor, hair fanned out behind her. She picked up a tendril of hair and let it curl around her finger, staring at it absent-mindedly.

"It's sad, though, about Lizzie's mom. Did you know she died?"

Cassie raised her head. "She's not dead. She moved to New York for work."

It was my turn to give Cassie a confused look. "She said her mom committed suicide, that her biggest fear was turning out like her."

With a snort of disbelief, Cassie's eyes widened and she sat up. "When did she tell you that?"

I felt a thump in my head. Like a weight crashing down. "She also told me you'd spread lies about her having sex with your brother's friends," I said.

"She told you *what*?"

"She said that your brother wanted to date her until you poisoned him against her."

Cassie's mouth hung open in shock. "Parker didn't want to date her because she's sloppy seconds. His friend Alex hooked up with her last Christmas. I didn't have to say *anything*. He'd never go for a girl like her."

My face flushed red. I winced at my own gullibility.

"She just told you those things to make you feel bad for her."

"But Emily and Vivian—"

Cassie snorted. "They go along with whatever Lizzie says."

Just like Eric, the Ravens had played me. With a shudder, I remembered how close I'd come to cutting Cassie's hair.

I'd told the Ravens the truth about my brother. What

if they figured out a way to use it against me? A knot of worry tightened in my stomach. What would Ms. Harrison do if she found out a meth addict was hanging around the gates?

Kick me out? Call Mom?

He was going to ruin things for me, and for himself, if he kept coming around. Had he thought I'd be able to protect him in the city? Hide food, clothes, and money for him in a stump? Rescue him from himself?

I was trying to save a drowning person. Eric, flailing and kicking, would pull me under too. I had to let go or neither of us would survive.

Tuesday, October 7, 9:50 p.m.
From: Devon

Who's the guy you've been seeing behind my
back? Don't lie. Word travels fast between RH
and Melton.
    Just tell me the truth.

Wednesday, October 8, 3:58 p.m.
From: Hope

There is no guy, I swear. It was my brother. He
surprised me and showed up at the gates of the
school. I didn't tell the girls he was my brother.
It's just really confusing to explain. I promise,
you are the ONLY guy in my life.

Wednesday, October 8, 6:35 p.m.
From: Devon

Your brother? I'm not an idiot. I thought we
had something special. You're just like the
other RH girls.

Wednesday, October 8, 6:38 p.m.
From: Hope

He's in trouble.
I only told people he was my BF so they'd stop
asking questions. What can I do to make you
believe me?

Wednesday, October 8, 6:40 p.m.
From: Devon

You need to do something to prove we are real.
That you love me. Will you do it? No matter
what it is?

Wednesday, October 8, 6:49 p.m.
From: Hope

You know I'd do anything for you.

Wednesday, October 8, 9:08 p.m.
From: Devon

Send me a sexy pic.

Wednesday, October 8. 10:02 p.m.
From: Hope

Sexy?

Wednesday, October 8, 10:11 p.m.
From: Devon

It's not a big deal. We love each other, right? It'll
be our secret.

ERIC

Hope stood on the other side of the gates. The bars cast a shadow across her face. One eye peeked out, the other stayed hidden. My notebook was rolled up in her hands. I took it from her as she passed it to me, careful that our fingers didn't touch. I didn't want to contaminate her with all the poison inside me.

"I don't know why I gave you that stupid thing," I said, embarrassed.

She shrugged. "It didn't make much sense to me anyway." Our conversation was stilted. We stood on either side of the fence, staring at each other.

It made me sad seeing her like this, trapped behind the fence. I wondered why I'd come. And then the surge of want hit me. Without her, there'd be no high tonight.

"You look good," she said. "Well, better."

I sniffed. I'd only had two minutes to wash away weeks of filth, but I'd left the shelter feeling like a new person. They'd given me new socks and underwear too. I'd locked up my jacket while I'd showered, to make sure no one stole it.

She gave a wan smile. "Where are you staying?"

Like it was a hotel. "With some friends. Pretty close to here, actually."

Her face softened, the guarded blankness in her eyes lifted. "Can I see it?"

I snorted a laugh of surprise. "I don't think you'd like it."

"You can't keep coming around. I'm going to get in trouble." She steeled herself, balling her little hands into fists, determined.

I waited for her to take it back, apologize. I was her brother, for Christ's sake.

"I'm not giving you money, Eric. I'm buying you food, and I want to see where you live." Her words came out in a rush, like they had been rehearsed.

"You sound like Mom," I told her, not trying to disguise the bitter edge in my voice. She was safe behind the bars, out of arm's reach. Would she have been so brave standing in front of me?

She set her mouth, determined.

"You're a bitch, you know that," I spat at her. She'd dangled money in front of me, tantalizing me with it. Only to snatch it away. I wanted to reach through the bars and grab her neck to shake it out of her.

She was crying now, wiping away tears. "I don't care what you think. I know what will happen if I give it to you. I know what you'll do with it."

I grabbed the bars and shook them. "Fuck you!" I yelled. "I don't want your fucking money!"

She didn't move. She was going to let me walk away, penniless.

Thrusting a hand through, I reached for her, beseeching. "Please, Hope! Just ten bucks. I swear, that's it, and then tomorrow, I'll come back, we can hang out. Do whatever you want. Please?"

She shook her head, feet rooted to the spot. "No. Come back on Saturday."

I let my hand drop and slid to the ground, staring at her, pressing my forehead against the cool metal. "I'll be dead by then. You'll have killed me, you know that, right? It's only ten fucking dollars. You don't even need it. You're just a selfish bitch." The words came out keening, like a dying animal.

She was immovable. I saw her tremble, like a volcano before it erupts. "Saturday," she said, her voice cracking. "Or no money."

I glared at her from the ground and then horked a wad of spit at her feet. I didn't need this shit. Little bitch of a sister trying to tell me what to do. Fuck that. "And fuck your fucking school, too!" I shouted. I wanted to throw something, but all I had was the notebook in my hands. I ripped off the cover and yanked pages from the staples, spewing them onto the sidewalk and through the gates.

They shone white in the darkness.

And I left.

HOPE

As he walked away, I tried to hold myself steady.

He had never wanted to see me. He had just wanted my money. The chance to get high. Nothing mattered but getting meth.

I felt like Mom, taking his abuse, letting it rain down on me and doing nothing. Suppressing a reaction, refusing to let him goad me into saying something I'd regret. But it had taken all of my energy. I should call Mom. I knew I should. She deserved to know Eric was still alive.

But she'd want to come to the city. She'd find him and tell the cops. Or worse, scare him off. Or be mad at me for not having called her sooner.

With the promise of my cash, he'd come back. He'd cool off and come back Saturday, apologetic, and try to woo it away from me. I didn't know if I'd be strong enough to say no the next time.

Some of his papers had blown under the gates and lay at my feet. I picked them up, eager to remove evidence of his visit.

I turned to go back inside the school. Lit from within, it looked homey in a weird way. The windows glowed against the brick exterior. Skeletal trees reached up to the sky like gnarled hands growing out of the earth. Movement in one of the windows made me stop. A group of girls was watching me from the third floor. The common room window.

Without any leaves on the trees, their line of sight was clear. They could have seen the whole thing. Eric railing against me, ripping up his book, and storming off.

To them, what had it looked like? A visit with my meth-head brother or a heated argument with my supposed boyfriend?

> Naked
> Flesh bared,
> Secrets of my soul
> Exposed.
> Cannibalize me.

The rush of words filled my head. Each footstep marked a syllable as I drew closer to the doors.

My stomach clenched because I knew Devon would find out. Gossip and rumours spread between our schools like social wildfire. It was only a matter of time before I got an accusatory text from him.

Devon, my heart cried. *You don't understand. Let me explain.* But already, I knew the thin reed of excuses I'd string together would bend and break under pressure. I'd have to tell him the truth.

A meth-head brother. Trailer trash family. A mom who thinks her daughter deserves better than she does.

Hope: a liar, a cheat, pretending to be someone she's not. How would I answer these accusations, when they were all true?

ERIC

*C*oach Williams. His name beat a rhythm in my head. Each step, a beat to his name. I'd tried to snort it away, block it, run from it, but nothing was working. As soon as the high wore off, my next thought was about getting more speed to erase what he'd done, what I'd done, from my memory.

I fantasized about seeing him again, in my highest moments. When I felt invincible. Tough. Sexy. Cool. I'd find him, proclaim him for what he was to the shock and horror of everyone watching. Vindication! I'd be whole again, able to function.

But that day was never going to come. Right now, I needed a hit. I'd beg Leo. Promise to give him some cash, whatever I got from Hope. I'd go back, meet her, let her buy me some food, and then sell it on the corner as soon as she left.

I was finding my way in the city. Learning how it worked. Go to the food bank, stand in line, pack a bag, say thank you, all meek and pathetic, and then scam five dollars for it on the corner. This was the way the real world worked.

Coach Duke Williams. I could find him. I could find out where he lived and pay him a visit for real. Show him what I'd become thanks to him. Everything was because of him.

Fuck. The word rolled through my brain in a long, slow syllable. All of this was because of him and he didn't even know it.

HOPE

I unbuttoned my blouse. The flesh on my chest was pale. Devon's necklace glinted against my skin. A tendril of hair fell over my shoulder and I peered into the camera. My heart was beating quickly. I'd locked the door after Cassie left for a tutoring appointment. But every time footsteps went past the door, I froze, terrified of getting caught. I knew what I was doing was wrong.

Pushing the thought out of my head, I took a deep breath and bit my bottom lip suggestively, staring into the camera. I tilted my head and unbuttoned my blouse so my bra was fully exposed. Letting the sleeves of my blouse slide down my arms, I slipped one bra strap off my shoulder and then the other, clutching the bra to my chest. My breasts heaved, their soft mounds of flesh pressing against my arm.

Devon had never asked anything of me before. He wanted this. I could give it to him. It would keep him with me, no matter what he found out about Eric. It would bring us closer. And that was what I wanted—to keep him close to me.

This wasn't so much, a few shots of me naked, my gift to him.

Pulling my arm away, I unhooked my bra and let it fall to my lap. I sat, exposed, a pouty look on my face, and felt the camera's eye capture my image, holding it. I took a couple more, letting my hair cover part of my face, half turning away from the camera, angling my head down, shyly, kissing the pendant he'd sent me, and biting it with a knowing smile.

My heart hammered in my chest as I perused the photos. It was weird, to look at myself like that. To know that with the click of a button, I'd be able to send them to someone else, secrets delivered, soul bared.

I saved the best ones in a file and deleted the rest. It was done now. I'd send them to Devon. He deserved them.

> Saturday, October 11, 11:22 a.m.
> **From:** Hope
>
> Do you like them? It felt so weird at first, but then I started thinking about everything you've done for me, getting me through the hard times at school, making me feel like someone cared when I felt alone. They're my thank-you gift to you.

> Saturday, October 11, 3:45 p.m.
> **From:** Devon
>
> You slut.

I reread the text.

Slut? Was he joking? My chest tightened. What had I done?

I dropped my head into my hands. I'd made a fool of myself. He'd never meant for me to send photos like that. My face burned scarlet. I was an idiot. He'd never speak to me again.

Oh my God, I'd ruined everything. Barely pausing to think, I ran to my computer and typed an email to salvage the only thing that mattered to me: my relationship with Devon.

> Saturday, October 11, 3:55 p.m.
> **To:** Devon
> **From:** Hope
> **Subject:** I'm an idiot
>
> Devon, please forgive me! I thought the photos
> were what you wanted, but I see now that I was
> wrong. Totally, totally wrong. I can't believe I
> sent them. I'm mortified. Please forgive me.
> Delete them and pretend they never existed.
> H.

I sat by my computer, phone in hand, for the rest of the night, waiting for the cheerful ping to announce I had a message. It never came.

ERIC

Hope had been crying. Her eyes were red and puffy. She walked out of the school with her hands stuffed into her pockets, hunched over, like she wanted to curl up into herself and disappear.

She didn't say anything to me, but the gates slid open and we were together again. No barrier between us.

I gave an awkward laugh. "They let you out."

"Only for an hour," she said, her voice quiet and small. "There's a grocery store a couple of blocks away."

I knew the place. A mom-and-pop joint with tiny shopping carts whose wheels twisted spastically. Bars on the windows and a sign that said NO PUBLIC TOILETS. I'd lifted a tin of tuna from there for me and Storm to share.

"The place you're staying, is it close?" she asked. A breeze rustled through her hair, swirling her ponytail behind her.

I cracked my knuckles, shaking my head. "I don't think you want to see it."

"That's the deal. The money is for food and I see where you live." Her face was serious, stern.

A silent, body-shaking groan rolled through me. "Why are you being such a bitch about this?"

Tears welled in her eyes, and her face flushed. Had she been crying because of me? *Fuck*. I didn't want this. Her pity or blame, or whatever emotions were going to roll through me when I looked at her.

I just wanted some cash. And, actually, some food wouldn't be so bad either. Once I was sober, the constant, gnawing hunger was exhausting. "Okay, okay, you can see the place. But I swear, Hope, if I find out you told Mom, or if you come back, I'll fucking leave. You will *never* see me again."

She took a deep breath and nodded. Why did she want to see where I crashed? For proof of how far I'd fallen? Anger swelled in me. She was stabbing needles into my eyeballs, forcing me to show her the flophouse. And I was willing to do it for twenty bucks.

"When did you get here, anyway?" she asked.

I snorted. "Don't know. Few weeks ago, I guess. Maybe less."

"Why'd you come to the city?"

Her questions set my teeth on edge. I didn't owe her an explanation. "Just needed a change," I said quietly, my voice tight with the memory of the pharmacy, the shrill blare of the alarm.

I thought seeing Hope this afternoon would be like old times, me and her. But she was ruining it with her interrogation. She'd left the bars of the school behind, but there was still a wall between us. She was guarded and didn't look at me, kept her head down, staring at the sidewalk.

"How's that school? You like it?"

Her chin quivered.

I frowned. An old protectiveness rose in me. "What happened?"

She shook her head, refusing to talk.

Two could play this game. "I'm not taking you to my place unless you come clean with *me*. Is it the other kids? Do you miss home? What?" It was a relief to turn the focus away from me, the fuck-up brother.

A few tears leaked down her cheeks, but she wiped them away. She had on black mini-mitts, the stretchy kind that made her hands look like small and rounded, like a kid had drawn them on. "I did something really stupid." Her voice broke. "I screwed everything up."

Without thinking, I put an arm around her shoulders, but she stiffened, so I dropped it. "What'd you do?" I asked. "Come on, you can tell me. It can't be as stupid as stuff I've done." Trying to make her laugh. It worked. A wry laugh interrupted her sobs.

She considered telling, I could tell, but then shook her head. "It's too humiliating," she whispered. "I can't tell you." She pulled away from me.

What could she have done, my little sister? Cheated on a test? Pissed off a teacher? Said something nasty about another girl? Her repertoire for bad behaviour was pretty slim.

"Did I tell you I have a dog?" I asked, changing the subject. "Storm. Found her on the side of the road. She's getting big now, but when I found her she was only a couple of weeks old."

Hope wiped her eyes and looked at me. "You always wanted a dog."

"She's smart. Already housebroken. You'll get to see her, when you come by the house."

She didn't say anything, just trudged ahead to the grocery store at the end of the street and went inside.

I pushed the cart though the aisles. It whined, one bum wheel wobbling, fighting me on the corners. Hope pointed out things I used to eat. Kraft Dinner, canned ravioli, sandwich meat. It all looked foreign— packaged and contained. It wasn't real. Whatever was behind the labels was just fake shit. What was real was scavenging, digging through garbage in a treasure hunt, working for a meal and eating whatever I found. *That* was real.

"Fucking cart." The wheel jammed when I tried to turn. I crashed into a bin of tuna, the cans rattling in their wire cage.

"Here, let me." Hope's hands appeared beside mine on the handle. Small and delicate. Next to hers, my hands looked massive, cut and scratched. The wound on my hand was still unhealed; the scab dark red with crusty edges. My fingernails, dirty, yellowed, and too long. I stuffed them into the pockets of my jacket and followed behind Hope like a scolded child.

Down the cereal aisle. Boxes of Corn Pops with NHL players taking slapshots on the front. Hope's eyes fell on the box with my favourite player, Darren Risk. She grabbed for it, but I told her no and put it back on the shelf, walking past the boxes quickly. I wanted to swipe them off the shelves and stomp on his face. Watch the Corn Pops explode out of boxes as I pummelled Darren's face to cardboard mush.

"Don't you miss it?" she asked a second later. Like the question had been weighing on her.

I shrugged. Hockey and Coach Williams were intertwined. Thinking about one meant thinking about the other. And without something to take the stabs of pain away, I didn't want to go there.

She pulled something out of her pocket. A piece of paper. My own handwriting. *Coach Williams* scrawled all over it twenty times. At the top, Hope had written a phone number and address. "There was only one Duke Williams in the phone book."

My heart thudded to a sharp stop in my chest, like someone was squeezing it.

He didn't want me to call him Coach when we were together. Then, it was *Duke*. He liked to hear me say it out loud when he was—

Bile rose in my throat.

"His name was in your notebook, over and over."

She'd misunderstood. I hadn't written it because I missed him, or wanted to see him again. I'd written it to excise the demons in my head, the ones that appeared at the thought of him.

And now, I had his number. His address.

"I called him. He said he'd like to see you. He meant it, Eric. I could tell."

She could tell? I fought for control. Not to run from the grocery store and keep running till my legs gave out, the bones liquefying with exertion.

"You talked to him?" I kept my voice even, but inside, I quaked. Split in two. The day he'd left Lumsville he'd texted me to say goodbye. "You're a special kid," he'd added at the end.

I was on meth by then, using it to lose myself, to feel better about who I'd become.

"He was surprised you were in the city. Thought you might have gone to a farm team this year. I"—she broke off—"I didn't tell him everything."

Like she was protecting me. And then she gave me a small, hopeful smile. "Do you think you'll call him?" she asked.

I stuffed the paper into my pocket. My mouth dry and my body screaming for a hit.

HOPE

He kept his promise. After the grocery store, we walked to the house he lived in. I stared at the outside of it and wanted to cry for him. Peeling gray paint, a roof that sagged with missing shingles. It looked like it was going to collapse on itself. The yard was scrubby with weeds and garbage. Plywood, covered in graffiti, hid the windows.

A guy walked by pushing a shopping cart loaded down with green garbage bags. Layers of clothes and a full beard concealed his body and face. I shuffled out of the way so he could pass. I held my breath but still caught a whiff of his urine-soaked clothes. The smell made me want to puke.

"Oh." Eric winced. "Shit. I forgot to get dog food for Storm." He looked at me. "She'll be hungry."

He didn't have money to feed himself, but he wanted to buy food for his dog. It made me shake my head. And then I caught myself, falling for his tricks.

"I don't have any more cash, Eric," I lied.

His mouth twisted into a scowl. "Did I ask you for any?"

I steeled myself for a string of abuse, but it didn't come. His shoulders stiffened with the effort.

My feet wouldn't move off the sidewalk. What would be inside? A stained mattress on the floor of his room? Junkies sleeping off their high? It was like the flophouses on the cop shows Dad watched.

Eric had already moved to the front door, expecting me to follow him.

"Eric," I called from the front steps. "Here, take the groceries. I'm going back to school."

"I thought you wanted to see inside," he said, a hint of "I told you so" in his voice.

I shook my head. "I can't. I told the school I'd only be gone an hour. I'll get in trouble." I couldn't bear to go inside, to have images of this house burned into my memory. To know this shithole was where my brother lived.

Maybe he saw the house through my eyes, catching a glimpse of my disgust. "I'm not going to be living here forever, you know." He narrowed his eyes defensively. "It's temporary."

"Mom's worried about you." I waited for a reaction, the inevitable explosion.

His face went cold. He stared at me.

"I promised her I'd let her know if I heard from you." I bit the insides of my mouth to keep from saying more.

He was across the yard in three steps, breathing in my face—hot, tangy, rancid. I flinched, cowering from the smell. "You fucking tell her and I'll disappear! You will never see me again. Ever!"

"Why?" I took a step back. "She just wants to know you're okay."

"NO!" he yelled. The tendons of his neck bulged. "You don't know what you're doing, Hope. You think you do, but you don't. Coach Williams, Mom—leave them the fuck out of my life."

"She told me what you did, why you left. Maybe if she knew you were sorry—" I hadn't finished talking before he was in my face, my arms mashed in his grip, squeezing so tightly it took my breath away.

"You don't know the half of what I did. You, Mom, Dick—none of you know shit about me, but you walk around pretending, like I could have been something."

I'd started to cry, terrified by his rage. "You're hurting me," I whimpered. The meth had wasted the fat from his body, but his muscles were still there, his grip still strong, bruising my arms.

His body trembled and he let go but grabbed my chin, twisted it around so I faced the house. "You see this? *This* is where I belong."

I shook my head. "No, it isn't." His fingers jammed my cheeks against my teeth. I could taste warm, metallic blood in my mouth.

"You know what Coach Williams told me once? That we get what we deserve. I thought he was talking about hockey, about trying hard, working for something." Spittle flew out of his mouth as he spat the words at me. "He wasn't talking about hockey," he hissed in my ear.

"Yo! Calvin!" A voice from the house. Eric's hands loosened. I shook him free and stumbled away from him. "What're you doing?" A guy had appeared on the front steps. He had long hair, his face hollow like Eric's, as if all the fat had been sucked out, leaving just skin and bones.

Eric froze. "I was just …" He stammered for an explanation. I didn't wait to hear what he said, or to find out why the guy called him Calvin. I took off, running back to school, putting as much distance between me and Eric as possible.

ERIC

Fuck me if Hope didn't take off. Like I was a freaking axe murderer.

"Who was that?" Leo asked when I pushed past him to get inside.

"My sister," I muttered, hauling the groceries into the kitchen. I held onto the edges of the kitchen table and took a deep breath. I hadn't meant to freak out on her. My hands ached with the feel of her twiggy little arms in them. *Fuck.* I should have reined it in. She didn't know.

I wished I'd told her when it first happened. But then she'd have to carry the burden too. I was torn between protecting her and myself. Now, neither of us was safe.

"Whoa, she bought you all that?" Leo followed me into the kitchen. He peered inside. "You going to keep it or sell it?"

Storm was at my feet, pawing at my leg for some attention. I opened the jar of peanut butter and scooped some onto my fingers. "Here, girl," I said and held it out to her.

"I never knew you had a sister. Never mentioned her before." Leo looked offended, the plastic bags rustling as he inspected their contents. Storm had licked away the peanut butter. A sticky film covered my fingers. I should have bought her some food. All this other stuff was going to make her sick.

"Yeah, well," I sighed. "She won't be coming back."

I'd seen how she ran away, scared I'd come after her. I'd made her afraid of me. Now I needed a hit more than ever. "I need to sell this shit. You coming?"

Leo shook his head. "Nah. But you should go to that alley behind the food bank. Everyone knows to go there if they want to buy stuff."

Hauling the groceries off the table, I took Storm with me, her leash in one hand. I spotted a guy I knew walking toward me on the sidewalk. He lived a block away, but didn't use. He'd stopped to pet Storm before, always asking first if she was friendly. "Hey, man. I got peanut butter for two dollars. You want?"

"The kind with all the crunchy shit in it?" he asked.

He dug out some change and I sold it to him for a dollar.

I didn't bother going to the alley, just set up shop right in front of the house, stretching my goods around me. Bag of potato chips, a loaf of bread, some KD, a tub of margarine to make the KD, and some milk and juice. I took a swig of juice before I put it up for sale. All I needed was ten dollars to get me through till tomorrow.

I dropped more change into my pocket as a guy walked away with the chips. A paper crinkled in my pocket and I pulled it out. Coach Williams' number.

Fuck me.

A thought rolled around in my head, not making sense, but persistent. I could go see him. Show up on his door and force him to admit what he did to me. Tell the cops.

But they'd arrest me for the pharmacy. I took another swig of juice, wiping my mouth with my sleeve.

A guy stood in front of me, pointing at everything left. "I got a kid. How much?"

"Five bucks," I told him. He whined and complained but passed the money over and walked away with a bag of groceries worth triple that.

I had enough to buy a hit that would last for a few hours. I'd be able to think clearly, work out the plan that was taking shape in my head.

HOPE

I hadn't slept. My arms, sore and bruised from where Eric had grabbed them, had made it impossible. His fingerprints all over me. I'd woken up early and spent too long in the shower, my skin now red and pulsing from the scalding water.

> I feel it all.
> Acutely
> Like fingernails bitten
> to the quick.
> Raw,
> Exposed skin quick to bleed.
> Nerves soft and
> tender.
> Unprotected.

The poem was written in a swirl on my palm. A reminder of what life with Eric was like. When I closed my fist, the words were hidden, held tight.

As I got dressed, I heard the ping of a new email. Please, please let it be Devon with a message of forgiveness.

Monday, October 13, 7:47 a.m.
To: Hope
Cc: #RH Students
From: Devon
Subject: Whore

Enjoy the pictures of Ravenhurst's stupidest slut
ever.

Shock slapped me in the face, then kicked me in the
stomach. I doubled over at my desk, gripping my sides. I
couldn't breathe. Every student at Ravenhurst was going to
wake up to photos of me topless, staring into the computer
and pouting like a fool, kissing the LOVE, DEVON pendant.

What would the Ravens do to me, once they saw the
photos? I started to tremble, too shocked to cry.

Devon wouldn't do this, not to me. We were together.
Thoughts ricocheted through my brain. What if it wasn't
him? What if someone had hacked his computer and
sent the pictures out? With fiery conviction, I wrung my
hands, squeezing my knuckles, trying to figure out what
to do. I had to talk to Devon!

I couldn't send an email. Whoever had hacked
his computer would intercept it. I grabbed my phone,
started to write a text, and stopped. What would I say?
No, I had to talk to him, find out what had happened.

I needed to hear his voice. With frantic fingers, I
searched online to find the phone number for Melton Prep.
I'd say there was a family emergency. My fingers shook so
badly, it took me three tries to punch in the number.

"Melton Preparatory Academy," the secretary
answered.

I cleared my throat. "I need to speak with Devon Huddington, please. It's an emergency."

"With whom?"

I repeated his name, my voice catching in my throat.

"Just a minute." She put me on hold, the phone making a repetitive beep as I waited, shivering and sweating at the same time.

"Hello," the secretary said, "Devon no longer attends Melton."

"What? Are you sure? Devon Huddington. H-u-d-d-i-n-g-t-o-n," I spelled for her. "He's in grade eleven." A swell of panic rose in my stomach.

"I remember him, but he no longer attends."

I froze with the phone in my hand. He'd lied to me? He didn't go to Melton? I couldn't make sense of it.

"Was there anything else?" she asked brusquely.

"N-no," I mumbled and hung up. My head started to throb. There had to be an explanation.

> Monday October 13, 8:02 a.m.
> **From:** Hope
>
> Please call me ASAP! Something horrible has happened.

I stared at my phone, waiting for it to answer me back. But nothing happened.

ERIC

I pulled out anything I could write on—the photos, Hope's old poems, the grocery receipt—and started a list. I had to make a list, while the plan was fresh in my head. I had so much to do.

The high was exhilarating. I was soaring over all my problems, sorting them out, making sense of them. God, it felt good not to be a victim. I couldn't believe it had taken me this long to figure out what I needed to do. Meth helped. Things made sense on meth.

My hand couldn't write fast enough to keep up with my brain. The list rat-a-tatted through my head, like machine-gun fire. I rewrote some of the things, they were important. And kept underlining them, so I'd remember.

Coach Williams. I wrote his phone number and address out over and over. I couldn't forget it: 314 Blossom Bay. I needed to find out where it was, how far away. One more thing to add to my list.

HOPE

Monday, October 13, 8:54 a.m.
From: Blocked number

Are you seriously this stupid? You are a slut and an idiot.

There is a Devon, but he was never interested in you. He doesn't even know you exist.

You probably wish you were dead, right? Now that you've put your tits on display for the whole world to see.

Guess what? We wish you were dead too. LOL.

Empty glass eyes stared at me. Devon's bear was perched on my pillow. *There was no Devon.* My mind kept spinning through the reality, trying to make sense of where the lies had started. I scrolled back through all the texts and emails, back to the very first one he'd sent.

No longer did I imagine Devon, a slight smile tugging at his lips as he typed a message to me. Nausea rose in me, burned its way up my throat. Who had it been on the other end of the computer, answering my emails, making me feel better, sharing my secrets?

The doorknob turned and I bolted out of my chair. Cassie, her hair wrapped in a turban and cheeks flushed from a shower, darted in and closed it quickly. She eyed me warily, as if I were a caged animal. Neither of us spoke.

Collapsing into my chair, I pressed my face into my hands. She knew. The photos were being passed around on cellphones all over the dormitory, everyone gawking at my nakedness and laughing at my stupidity.

The necklace from Devon still hung around my neck. I tried to yank it off, pulling so hard the back of my neck burned in pain. The chain dug in, refusing to break. With a frustrated cry, I tried to unclasp it, but my hands were shaking and I gave up. Maybe it was better to leave it on as a tangible remembrance of what an idiot I was.

I heard Cassie behind me, stuffing her toiletries bag onto her shelf, hanging her robe on its hook. "The shower room's empty, if you want to use it." Her voice came from a million miles away.

My chin quivered, but I shook my head. "I can't."

"They're not that bad," she said.

Stupid, sweet Cassie with her blond curls and scratch-the-surface-and-you're-through personality. If only my biggest problem was what my breasts looked like.

She started to bustle around the room, digging out knee-highs and a blouse. "Really, something else will happen and everyone will lose interest in a day or two, you'll see."

I shook my head and stared at her.

It was so much worse than just the photos. I'd clung to Devon, desperately. He was the only friend I had at Ravenhurst. I'd shared secrets with him, made myself vulnerable. I'd let him know me in a way no one else had. I'd sent him the photos because I trusted him.

And now, he was gone.

> Falling
> Tumbling
> Wind rushing past my ears
> I plummet to your waiting arms.
> But you are a
> Figment.
> And you disappear as I
> Crash.

If Devon didn't exist, who'd been on the other side of the computer answering my emails? Whose cellphone had I been texting?

The slash of Lizzie's lipstick, scarlet against her pale skin, flashed into my head and I felt myself shrivel. When Devon had asked how I really felt about the Ravens, I'd told him, exaggerating stories and making snarky comments. He'd eaten it up, encouraging me in our united distaste for them. I'd fed into it, and each email had dug me into a deeper hole. My stomach gave a sickening drop. I'd given them a reason to hate me.

ERIC

I was at the gates again, clamouring for Hope. The guard knew me. "I'll get her," he said into the intercom.

I'd sold my jacket. The one Hope had given me. Spit-polished the scuff marks off and brought it down to a pawn shop. The guy behind the counter had given me fifty bucks. He'd kept a poker face, but I'd assured him it was expensive. Good deal for him. Someone had probably already bought it now that the days were getting colder.

Even high, I'd felt a pang when I'd left the shop, the security door clicking shut behind me. I remembered the day I'd found it, hidden in the tree stump. Hope had already left by then. I'd never thought I'd come all this way to find her.

But I needed cash. I had to be high for my plan to work, and I needed supplies. Leo found a jacket for me to wear, plaid flannel on the outside, like a lumberjack's. I'd left it behind at the house, he told me. He'd been saving it in case I came back.

I had to wait a while until Hope ran out of the building to the gates, her hair flying behind her. I didn't think she'd come, to be honest, after the way she'd torn off the other day. I paced back and forth across the driveway, waiting for her to make her way to me. Jolts of energy shot through me, making my fingers wiggle like I was playing the piano. I jumped up and down a few times, the bottoms of my feet shooting out rocket blasts.

"Eric." Her voice was desperate, breathless. "You have to help me."

I looked at her. In the darkness, I couldn't see her face clearly.

"I need to leave. I have to go home."

I wanted so bad for my mind to focus on her, to latch on to her words, but it kept shooting off to something else, the real reason I was here.

"Okay, okay. We can go. I'll take you, that's no problem. Hey, here's the thing, though." The ideas shot through my head like fireworks, arcing in my mind with a trail of flame. "I can't leave yet. There's something I need to do. I can't let him get away with this. You get what you deserve, just like he told me."

She leaned against the bars. "Eric, please!" she begged. "Just help me get home. Take me to the bus station. Is that how you got here? By bus?"

"Nah! I hitched." A memory of the trucker, of what I'd had to do. It all got jumbled up. "I will help you. We can leave tomorrow, I promise. I just have to do something first and it has to be dark. Not tonight. I don't have all the shit I'm going to need."

"What? What do you need? What are you going to do?"

I laughed. "Yeah, you'd like to know. But I'm not going to tell you." I shook my head at her. Then got real close to the gates, my hands wrapped around the cold metal. "It's all right here." I tapped my head. "And here." I pulled out my list, the one in my back pocket, and showed it to her. She couldn't read anything in the darkness, but she squinted at it.

"What if I help you? Can we do it together?"

I rocked back and forth. All this fucking energy coursed through me, like at a speedway, the cars going up and down each limb.

"What are you doing?"

I didn't know. Maybe making car engine noises? My lips were vibrating.

"Here, take it." I passed her the paper. "It's the list of supplies. Get everything on it and I'll come back tomorrow. We can do it together and then I'll help you."

Hope's eyes were big. I could see the whites of them glowing. "Eric." She grabbed my hand, holding me to her. Her hands were cold too, but not as cold as the metal. Her skin was soft over her bones. "I can't stay here. If you don't come back for me tomorrow, I'll leave without you." The sound of her voice hammered at me. I knew it mattered what she was saying. I tried hard to hold on to it, the message in her words, but it flew away from me, escaping.

I had to go. There was still so much to do. At the corner, I felt in my pocket for the list, but it was gone.

Had I given it to Hope? Had she stolen it? Had I dropped it? I didn't have time to look for it. I'd make another one at home and keep planning.

There was a lot to do before tomorrow night.

HOPE

My alarm buzzed me to consciousness at 5:00 a.m. Half-asleep, I felt for the button, slamming my hand on the nightstand. Within seconds, reality crashed down on me. Flashes of the images that had been emailed back to me, to every student at Ravenhurst and probably Melton, burst into my head. I pulled my pillow tight around my ears, pressing my nose into the mattress and wishing I could suffocate myself.

I'd gone to bed last night hoping I'd die in my sleep.

The incessant bleeping of the alarm started again. I'd only pressed the snooze button. Cassie mumbled in her sleep, and I forced myself to wake up. I grabbed my towel and robe. If I got to the shower room before the other girls, I could enjoy a few minutes of peace. Once the rest of them were awake, I'd have to endure whispered comments and looks of disgust. Unlocking the door, I shut it gently behind me, careful not to wake Cassie. The chill of the hallway made goosebumps rise up my legs. I turned back to get my slippers. WHORE had been scrawled across my door in red lipstick.

I closed my eyes and when I opened them, the word was still there.

With manic determination, I used my towel to wipe it off, smearing the scarlet grease across the door. My arm and shoulder burned from exertion, but I kept rubbing. The letters faded, tinting the door pink, but couldn't be erased.

ERIC

I'd had to ask for directions a few times, but now I stood in front of 314 Blossom Bay, with the sun rising behind it. Pumpkins lined the steps and a scarecrow stared at me from a flower bed. Every house looked the same in this neighbourhood, except for the Halloween decorations. Storm squatted, taking a dump on the boulevard.

A plastic bag of supplies swung against my leg. Like in an Easter egg hunt, I'd found them all, my brain jumping from spot to spot until I had what I needed. Rags, gasoline, bottles. Bought with what was left of the money from selling my jacket and scavenged from garbage bins. I hadn't needed Hope's help after all.

I'd walked here. It had taken hours. At first, I'd felt like I was flying—meth gave me energy—but now the high was wearing off and all I wanted to do was crash. The sun was rising, making the sky glow orange, like it was on fire.

It was a new day.

I'd passed a park with a lake in the middle of it. Maybe I'd find a bench and sleep for a while. My attention went back to Coach Williams' house when a light went on in a room upstairs. My heart stuttered in my chest. He was home.

My bravery disappeared. I was just a shell again, trembling at the thought of seeing Coach Williams.

You're not like the other guys. You've got talent. Real talent. I've been talking to friends of mine, coaches who could make things happen for you, Eric. Hey, do me a favour, when it's just us, call me Duke, okay?

Scouts came out. I could have made it, gone pro. Coach Williams had me believe it was all happening because of him. We were a team. I had to keep him close, or my future would fall apart. And I'd believed him.

Come on, have a beer. You need to relax. You like porn, right? Nothing wrong with a bit of pussy and cock. With the sounds of the movie in the background, he'd moaned, unzipped his pants, and taken out his dick, starting to rub it in front of me, like I wasn't there. *It feels good, doesn't it?* I'd looked away, too freaked out to leave. Trapped in the room with him.

I was still trapped. What he'd done sealed me into this life.

I wanted out.

HOPE

I moved through the day like a ghost, skimming down the corridor and sliding into my seat for classes and then disappearing to my room.

The other girls whispered when I walked past, or ignored me like I was something dirty. Even Cassie didn't want to talk to me in public, for fear she'd be tainted by me. By what I'd done.

Eric's list, the paper he'd given me yesterday, sat on my desk. I hadn't read it last night. He'd been talking like a crazy person, moving like his limbs were elastic bands, stretching and contracting. I just wanted him to listen to me. He needed to help me get out of this place.

Part of me knew I should call Mom, but that meant explaining what had happened. How could I tell her I'd sent naked photos of myself to someone I'd never met, a guy who'd professed his love for me? It was too humiliating. But if I left school, showed up at home, and blamed Eric, saying he'd shown up at school, hounding me, threatening me, making it impossible to live there, she'd let me stay. She'd understand the shame.

But she'd also come to the city looking for him. And then what? Tell the cops? Could I betray my brother that way?

A bag was packed, waiting, under my bed. I stared out the window, my eyes trained on the gates, straining to see in the darkness. *Eric,* I silently moaned, *don't let me down.*

But at ten minutes to lights out, dreams of having him whisk me to the bus station, saving me from this school and the Ravens, faded. He wasn't coming. Nothing I'd said yesterday had mattered to him.

I didn't matter to him. Tears burned in my eyes. After everything I'd done for him. I swallowed back a lump in my throat. Why was I surprised? The Eric who would have come back for me was gone, destroyed by meth.

Cassie came in and dumped books onto her desk. She'd been in the common room studying, avoiding me. The dorm felt claustrophobic with both of us in it. Without a word, I grabbed my toiletries bag and went to the shower room.

So close to lights out, the shower room was empty. I took off my robe and hung it on the hook. Finally, hiding myself in the steamy cubicle, uninterrupted tears ran down my face. They mingled with the shower spray and slid to the drain, escaping.

Shivering against the instant chill when I shut the faucet off, I reached for my towel and wrapped it around my body. A row of mirrors across from the stalls usually buzzed with chatter as girls stood combing their hair and slathering lotion onto their legs. But at this time of night, it was eerily silent, the row of globe-shaped bulbs glowing just for me. The drip of the shower echoed in the empty room.

My robe hung on a hook by the door. I slipped it on and felt something in the pocket.

I reached in and pulled out one of the photos of me, naked, the necklace dangling between my exposed breasts. Breath caught in my throat at the shock of seeing it, of knowing it was me. Crumpling it up, I threw it into the garbage can. The plastic lid swung open, accepting and thanking me for my offering. Nausea rose in my throat as I spun around, checking to see if anyone else was in the shower room.

Pushing the door open slowly, I edged into the corridor. It was empty. I had to make it to my room at the end, which meant going past Lizzie's room. Had she put the picture in my pocket? Or sent one of the other girls, the same way she'd tried to recruit me to cut Cassie's hair? Holding up the bottom of my robe so I could run, I sprinted to the end of the hall and turned the doorknob. It rattled, but the door didn't move. Staring at it in disbelief, I tried to turn the knob again. "Cassie!" I whispered, my voice a desperate sob. "Cassie!" There was no answer.

I felt myself weaken. She'd locked me out.

It was all too much. The constant snickers, the nasty comments, the glances my way; I had been humiliated, but to the Ravens it was a game. I was like a plaything to be batted around. Their razor-sharp claws had torn me to shreds.

"Cassie!" I called, now hammering on the door. "Open the door!" My yells woke other girls, who burst into the hallway, scowling at the disturbance. Why wouldn't she open it? I twisted the knob, kicked the bottom of the door, panic turning to anger.

A hand landed on my shoulder and I jumped, startled by the touch, and spun around. Ms. Harrison frowned at me. "Hope! You've woken the whole floor." Behind her, I could see Lizzie and the other Ravens, stifling giggles with their hands. Ms. Harrison rapped on the door with her knuckles. No answer. With an irritated sigh, she pulled a ring of keys out of her pocket and opened the door. There was Cassie, lying on her bed, one foot crossed over a knee, swinging to the beat of a song blaring into her earbuds.

Ms. Harrison stomped in, and to the amusement of the other girls, gave Cassie the fright of her life when she snatched the earbuds away. "Cassie," she admonished. "Hope was locked out. She was banging on the door."

Cassie, her eyes wide and startled, shook her head. "I didn't hear her."

"I know." Ms. Harrison spun around to the rest of us. "Back to bed, all of you." As the other girls slunk off, she pulled me aside. "Next time, just come and get me."

My face flushed with embarrassment. "Sorry."

"Off to bed, then," she said and with a brusque nod, closed the door. I could feel Cassie looking at me but ignored her, pulling on my pajamas with shaking hands.

"Sorry," she said. "I would have opened the door if I knew you were out there."

I ignored her and climbed into bed, pulling my legs up to my chest and curling up under the covers.

Tears leaked out of the corners of my eyes and ran onto the pillow.

Eric hadn't shown. Devon didn't exist. Everyone at school had turned their backs on me.

I had never felt so alone.

ERIC

When I woke up, I didn't know where I was or what time it was. I rolled over and almost fell onto the ground, the gravel path inches from my face. Storm was sleeping in the grass beside me. She raised her head, cocking it, one floppy ear pricked.

Fuck. I sat with my head in my hands, trying to piece the last hours together. I'd fallen asleep with the sun rising, and now it was setting. At the end of the bench, a brown lunch bag. GOD BLESS written in block letters. I picked it up. Inside, a sandwich wrapped in plastic, tightly so the bread bulged, a juice box, an apple, and a granola bar.

I ripped into the plastic, tearing it so the sandwich popped out, as if grateful for release.

Stuffing it into my mouth, I looked around. Fake lake, cookie-cutter houses covered in stucco, spindly trees. With a jolt, I remembered where I was.

Coach Williams. My bag of supplies. I jumped up, looking for it. There, under the bench. It was safe. I let out a relieved sigh.

I'd come all this way.

I'm not a fag, you know. What we do here, it doesn't make us homos. Here, let me show you how good it feels. You've never done this before, have you?

The sandwich rose in my throat. Undigested chunks made me gag.

I sat on the bench, my mind reeling, bouncing like a pinball. I couldn't let him get away with what he'd done to me.

But—sober—the plan was scary, crazy even.

He'd pushed me to this. *You get what you deserve.* I looked down at my dirty jeans, ripped and baggy, my shirt—washed once in weeks—rank with stink and sweat, and wondered if this was what I deserved.

I caught myself picking at the scab on my arm. Blood seeped out from under the crust of brown. It was never going to heal.

Just like me.

Storm nosed my leg and sat, waiting for a handout. Quietly quivering with anticipation.

I ripped off half the sandwich and gave it to her. Her sharp, white baby teeth dug into it. I kept my fingers close to her mouth on purpose. One of her teeth pierced my skin. I wanted the hurt to flow through me. I wanted to feel something different from hunger, exhaustion, and ache. But the sting was too small and stopped at my knuckle, like a paper cut. Nothing to leave a mark.

I bent down and rubbed her neck as she ate, gobbling it up. A piece of meat hung from the side of her mouth. I'd dragged her all over the city and now here: 314 Blossom Bay.

I slid down beside her, and she climbed onto my lap and licked my chin. I never should have brought her with me. A new feeling came on like a wave, rolling through me. Sadness. I clutched her to me, feeling her soft puppy fur, the silky underside of her ear, her rough, wet nose. I could hug her close, squish her against me, and feel her heart beating fast. She looked at me, so innocent, happy to follow. Too stupid to know not to.

The lake was in front of me, at the end of the paved path. I could take her down, hold her under, and wait until she stopped struggling. It was what the asshole who'd left her on the side of the road should have done in the first place. A kinder end than letting her starve in a box.

If I wasn't around to look after her, how long would she survive? She could get hit by a car or get picked up by the pound. Maybe it was kinder to end things for her now.

I held her against me, resting my head on her delicate skull. I unclipped the leash from her collar. It would be over quickly. I'd wade out and hold her under, let her body float out into the lake.

But then she squirmed in my arms and looked at me. Her eyes deep brown, like maple syrup.

Voices rang out across the lake. Kids playing, their heads bouncing above the fence on a trampoline. Flying. Weightless for a nanosecond. I had forgotten what that felt like. I stood up, holding Storm close, the warmth of her protecting me from the searing pain in my chest.

HOPE

Devilish thoughts
Turn black
Decay
Charred remains
Of what was loved
Now lie dead.

I'd avoided his stupid list. Leaving it in my desk drawer so I wouldn't have to look at it, but too mad to throw it away. Why did I think I could count on him? All he did was let me down. I should call Mom, let her call the cops or come to the city. It would serve him right.

But all those thoughts got mixed up with the shame I felt about the pictures; how eager I was to believe "Devon" loved me. A blurry mess. I couldn't keep straight who I hated more: Lizzie and the Ravens for their cruelty, Eric for his addiction, or myself for falling victim to their tricks.

I caught my reflection in the mirror. Like a hunted animal, my eyes wide and anxious, shoulders hunched to my ears. After a few minutes, I took a deep breath.

Hiking up my skirt, I grabbed a marker. The skin on my inner thigh was pale. Innocent.

> With a black heart
> Hiding
> One prick to pierce
> Your lies.
> You sizzle in your own flame.

I put the cap back on the marker and stared at what I'd written. Shockingly dark, it would be a reminder. And a promise.

Some chickadees, small and round, flitted from branch to branch in the tree at my window, chirping in a high-pitched singsong. The blackbird hadn't been by in days. Maybe the little birds had kicked him out.

I took Eric's list out of my drawer and stared at it. Folded so many times, the creases were furry. His printing, in dull pencil, was loopy and unformed. Kind of like Eric.

MATCHES (Leo has TIN in kitchen—take some!!!!)

Rags, dishtowels, sheets???? Ask Hope!

Gasoline (take old container from behind house and fill up at gas station. Save MONEY. Make sure I have enough!!!!)

Bottles. EASY to get! Look in garbage, recycling bins! Get 5!!! Or more!

MAP—how to get there? How to get there? How to get there?

314 Blossom Bay!!!!

Has to be nighttime when he's sleeping! Must be HOME! Otherwise, no point.

I stared at his words. His hockey coach's address? None of it made sense. Matches and gasoline? What was he going to do, burn down a house? And what did it have to do with Coach Williams?

What was going on in his twisted, junkie brain? I turned the paper over. On the back, *You get what you deserve*, written over and over, like a mantra.

He'd put it on me, again. I had to sort out what he was going to do and save him from himself.

It was almost six o'clock. The sun was setting, burning the sky orange and red. He'd abandoned me yesterday, when I had been counting on him. Was it because he was high somewhere, too blitzed on meth to remember his promise?

I hate you, Eric. A surge of anger rushed through me. He deserved to be locked up. His plan didn't make sense to me. Gasoline, bottles, Coach Williams: the ravings of a crazy person. But the fear of what he'd do, to himself, to someone else, was always in the back of my mind. What if he hurt an innocent person? I looked at the paper again. At the intensity of the words, written in capitals and underlined. Whatever his plan was, to his meth-addled mind, it made sense.

He'd need money to buy gasoline, I reasoned. And he hadn't asked for any. I thought back to the other night, plucking at strands of our conversation. Why hadn't he asked for any?

He'd been jumping around, frenetic, in a T-shirt, while I'd been shivering in the October air. His jacket. The one I'd left for him in Lumsville had been sold, pawned, probably, for half its value. Months of babysitting money wasted on a gift that wasn't as special as a few hits of meth. Or a misguided revenge plot.

My head throbbed, the ache starting at the base of my spine with the realization that I should have called Mom weeks ago, when Eric first showed up. I'd thought I could do it on my own, that some sibling magnetism would pull him to me. But I'd failed.

I stared at his coach's address. I'd given it to Eric, planted the seed in his head. Had the meth helped it bloom? Vines of ideas taking over his brain, strangling reason with their tendrils? His writing might be nothing, just the lunatic scribblings of a meth-head.

Or not. They could be real.

A hot rush of panic filled me and I picked up my phone. I couldn't fix Eric. But I couldn't let him hurt anyone else, either.

Please be home, I whispered. And then another thought: *Please don't let it be too late*.

ERIC

The glass bottles clinked in the bag, heavy with gasoline. Vapours rose around me, giving me a headache. No back lanes in this neighborhood, so I huddled in the shadows between houses.

I had to do this. I had to send a message that he couldn't get away with what he'd done to me. No deed goes unpunished. You get what you deserve.

Would we be even after this? Would I magically be healed, give up the meth? I knew I wouldn't. I still wanted it. Even now, sitting crouched by a basement window well, I wanted some crystal so bad my body crawled with the need of it.

Would the fire fill me up? Watching it blaze, would it burn inside of me too, scorching me into cinders? I already felt like ash, ready to blow away, dust on the wind. Maybe I should walk into it. Burn with him. Maybe that's where I belonged: with my dad and Coach Williams.

Maybe we were all versions of the same shitty person, just waiting for hell to take us.

HOPE

I stared at the poem on my leg. My head buzzed with unshed words. I needed my journal, but it wasn't in my nightstand drawer, or under my pillow, or anywhere else I usually left it. Opening all the drawers of my desk, I floundered around trying to remember when I'd last had it. Had I brought it to study hall? Stuffed it into my binder? How could I have lost it? I went through my pile of textbooks, lifting up each one to see if it had gotten trapped underneath.

A picture of unearthly, peachy skin sat tucked between the books. It was another picture of me, one of the ones I'd sent to Devon. The pendant held up to my lips. My eyes, disgustingly wanting. So much flesh exposed.

Seeing myself like that, the shock of another photo waiting for me, made me stumble backwards. I held the paper in my hand and collapsed onto my bed. How had it gotten there? In study hall? Or had Lizzie been in my room?

Were there other photos? Hidden, lying in wait until I found them? Like a carnival funhouse, the ghouls would pop up. An uninvited reminder of what I'd done.

My journal forgotten, I got up and opened dresser drawers, rifling through my clothes, tossing them to the ground. Where would other pictures be? Under my mattress? In my desk? I tore through everywhere, dumping books off shelves and the contents of desk drawers on the floor.

When I was done, my room looked like a hurricane had come through. My mattress was tipped over; clothes, books, papers strewn across the floor. I'd stripped off my hoodie, too heavy for strenuous work, and my hair hung in a straggly mess around my face. A bottle of painkillers from my toiletries bag rolled on the floor at my feet.

Pills rattled inside when I picked it up, fingering the ridges on the cap. I unscrewed it. With a shaking hand, the pills tumbled into my hand. Nestled in my palm, I counted twenty-two dots of chalky white. Would that be enough?

There was laughter outside the door. Girls in the hallway, the common room; they were everywhere, pressing from all sides, unavoidable.

A strangled scream lodged itself in my throat. What would they do if they found me in here, amidst the chaos I'd created? I glanced at the lock on the door, the button pressed in; all that protected me from the Ravens outside. The empty bottle in one hand, the pills in the other. If I popped them into my mouth, what then? Float away, my head like helium, wispy and free? No more pictures, no more Ravens, no more humiliation. No more being alone. No more hurt. I could escape. Maybe taking these pills was the only way out.

I put all the pills in at once, forcing my dry mouth to swallow them, my throat to contract as I pushed them down. The pills lodged in my esophagus, saliva dissolving them, their molecules slipping into my blood.

I waited. Shut my eyes and thought of Mom. She'd arrive, and then what? Come to my room to get me. See this. My eyes flew open. I staggered back—not from the pills but from the weight of what I'd done.

Rushing to the garbage can, I put my finger down my throat. I gagged, and the pills came up in a mass of bubbly spit.

I crouched on the floor, breathing hard. What was I doing? I couldn't let the Ravens win, not like this. I needed air. Wrenching the window open, I was hit by a blast of October air. It lifted the suffocating weight of the room. I gulped the air in. A bird's squawk startled me. Sitting on the branch beside my window, the blackbird had returned. It opened its beak again and cawed at me. I took a step back and it flew to the sill. Large, with greasy feathers, the crow's yellow eyes stared at me.

> Black beak
> Quick tap
> Flesh supple, like ripe fruit.
> Talons dig into my skin,
> Gripping and sinking.
> Peck viciously, madly
> Until my eye is an empty socket.

Eric's plan lay on the desk in front of me. His insistent scrawl a scream. The bird tilted its head at me.

Squeezing my eyes shut, I gripped the edge of the desk and took deep breaths. The room spun and I sank down to the floor, holding my head in my hands. What if I didn't go to him? What if I just let things happen? What then?

From outside my door, I heard a squawk—only it wasn't a bird, it was a Raven.

The one on the windowsill answered. Lifted its head and opened its beak with a caw. I wished it would fly inside the room. I glared at it, imagining what I would do if I had it in my hands.

> Skull between my fingers,
> I mash.
> Beak cracks, splinters
> A mass of feathers
> Falls to the floor.
> I press it flat,
> Raven dust
> Trailing under the door
> Like smoke.
> It disappears.

I wasn't going to be another victim. I'd left Lumsville to find a place where I fit in, that made sense for me. To escape Eric. Going back meant giving up, resigning myself to the idea that this was all my life would be.

I'd seen what giving up had done to Eric. One taste of meth and he'd let go. Everything that mattered to him had slipped through his fingers: family, hockey, friends. That wasn't going to happen to me.

"Go!" I yelled at the bird. It flew off in a mess of flapping feathers. I slammed the window shut and looked around my room. My computer sat on my desk, beside Eric's plans, and under it, my journal. It had been there all along. I gave a sigh of relief.

I knew what I was going to do. My plan was concrete in my head. Solid.

Two could play at Lizzie's game. She'd used my innocence against me. I'd use hers. She thought a computer brought her anonymity, but it didn't. From the privacy of my dorm room, with my computer open in front of me, I'd make sure I didn't go down without a fight.

ERIC

He was inside. I watched him move around the house, his shadow behind the blinds, a glimpse of him going upstairs, picking up a little girl in pink pajamas.

How long had I been sitting outside? Maybe if I stayed here, I'd sink into the ground and disappear. Decompose.

I wished I'd gone to see Hope. She'd have talked me out of this. But now I was here. And completely fucking confused.

He had a family. A wife and a kid.

What was I? A weird bruise in his past that had faded. Or were there others? Was he still coaching? Maybe a whole string of boys were in line behind me, working up the guts to do what I wanted to do.

I could write a letter and leave it where his wife would find it. Then she'd know what he really was. Take their kid and divorce him.

Taking out one of the bottles, already stuffed with a ripped-up rag, the gasoline sloshing inside, I held it in my hands. How easy would it be to light it and throw it and then walk away?

I wanted to hear him scream, terrified, like I had, the first time.

See how it feels, Coach Williams.

HOPE

My fingers trembled, racing to finish what I'd started. I had to find Eric, but first, I had to do this. I wasn't leaving Ravenhurst like a hunted animal. In fact, I wasn't leaving Ravenhurst at all.

I'd tell them everything, show them the photos, let them read the emails and texts, lay all my secrets bare so they'd know the truth.

Lizzie wouldn't be able to hide anymore. And neither would I.

A cluster of girls sat in the common room. I had to walk past them to make my way to the gates. It was night, late to be leaving the school.

"Where are you going?" Lizzie asked, looking up from her phone. She gave me a wicked smile. "Going to meet your meth-head brother?"

Any chatter in the room died with her words. I'd been waiting for her to unleash this final nail in my coffin. She'd known the truth about Eric since the first night I'd gone to her room, but only now, when she'd exhausted her arsenal of tricks, was she resorting to using it. I forced myself not to react and took a deep breath.

"Or maybe you're going to meet your boyfriend," she said quietly, so only I could hear. "*Devon*." Hearing his name on her lips, dripping with sarcasm, was like an ice pick through my heart. It took every ounce of self-control not to launch myself across the room at her.

"You think you won, don't you?" I truly wanted to know. Why was she like this? Manipulative and cruel, forcing people to dark places. She must have gotten some satisfaction from it.

She just arched a condescending eyebrow and picked up her phone.

"There should be an email in your inbox, Lizzie. I sent it to Ms. Harrison and copied you on it. A string of emails between me and Devon. All of them." Her expression didn't change. Nothing I said scared her.

"So? Those emails have nothing to do with me."

I trembled, a hot flush spreading up my cheeks. *Don't back down.* "I did some research. Whoever sent out those photos can be charged with distribution of pornography." A flicker of concern flashed across her face. "There's a whole team who can figure out the IP address of anyone who uses the Internet. Whoever did send the photos will be getting a visit from the police."

She gaped at me, speechless.

"And yes, I *am* going to see my meth-head brother," I whispered to her. "And then"—I leaned in close—"I'm coming back to Ravenhurst, because you don't get to win." I slung my backpack over my shoulder, my footsteps loud in the silent room. I met Cassie's eyes, wide with shock, and gave her a jubilant smile.

The security guard buzzed me out right away. Mom's car was parked at the end of the driveway, blinding me with its headlights.

ERIC

And then a car. A familiar car in unfamiliar surroundings. Out of context, it was like a dream. Maybe I was imagining it.

And then a voice. Someone was calling my name, shouting it across the street.

It was Hope.

They'd left. An hour ago, Coach Williams' car had reversed out of the garage. His wife sat beside him in the front seat and, in the back, his little girl. I'd stood and watched, paralyzed. The car moved slowly, cautiously to the road. I could have called to him then, ran to the street, broken the months of silence. But I'd stood mute, frozen in the darkness between houses.

I closed my eyes and felt Hope's hand on my arm, squeezing. Tears rolled down my cheeks. And then a loud, low moan as I fell against her. She pried the plastic bag of Molotov cocktails out of my hand, like a mother coaxing a toy from a child.

Tiny Hope, my body curled up against hers. Her bones felt as fragile as a bird's, but still she was holding me up.

"I couldn't do it," I sobbed. "I wanted to, but I couldn't."

She sat quietly, rubbing my back, like Mom used to do.

"The fucked-up thing is, I wanted to see him. It felt good to see him." My words were garbled, chewed up by emotion.

"I called them," she whispered. "I told them to leave. I didn't know what you were going to do, or why."

I squeezed my hand into a fist and jammed it into the ground. The soil was packed down, solid under my knuckles, but there was give there, a release as the earth cracked under my weight.

"He left," I spat, shaking my head. "You see that?" I pointed at the house, now encased in darkness. "An innocent man would've stayed."

Hope's face fell. She took in the broken shell of a person that sat in front of her and she crumbled. She clutched me, held me close, and I felt her body shake with sobs.

I heard another car door slam. Mom. She sank down beside us, gripping me.

Not letting go.

HOPE

Broken,
My brother sits beside me
Twisted and used, both of us.
Tangled together
We will find our way
Jumping over
Remnants of our lives,
Making a new path
Together.

ERIC

There are things I never saw before. The way the snow piles on branches of trees, threatening to spill off in a gust of wind. How the sky glows with colour in the morning and how snow sparkles in the moonlight. I catch myself noticing these things, like out-of-body visions, and shake my head. I'm no poet, not like Hope, but part of me wants to capture those moments, savour them.

All of this I see through the window of my room. I stare out of it for hours, letting my mind drift. Twenty-eight days in a hospital, sixty-seven days and counting as an outpatient, and I still crave the high meth gave me, gritting my teeth sometimes for the want of it. Some days, I miss it like a friend who's died, mourning its absence. And other days, I fly into rages, ranting against what it did to me. I don't remember the ugly days and nights of withdrawal in the hospital, and I won't let Mom tell me about them. It's all just a fog of pain now, a black hole I don't ever want to go back into.

Mom rented an apartment in the city. Close to Hope and close to the hospital. A furnished place, nothing in it feels like ours. We're just placeholders, waiting in limbo until I get back to normal. Normal: a finish line that's always out of reach. Richard drives in on weekends. It's hard for him to look at me sometimes. I see him holding his fork tightly at dinner, angrily chewing his food and biting back comments. Mom says he'll come around, but it takes times to forgive.

And forever to forget, I want to add.

I'm trying to move on, face what happened, but the meth left me with paranoia. I hear noises in the night and every time I leave the apartment, I look behind me, convinced I'm being followed. People from my past pop up in unexpected places: closets, cupboards, frozen-food aisles of grocery stores. My breath comes fast and my rational self explains them away. But always, there's hunger for something to take away the fear.

Through the thin walls of the apartment, I hear Mom on the phone. Her voice rises and falls in an unnatural cadence. "Eric!" she calls. "Eric!" Her voice is urgent. I peel myself off the bed and open the door. She's there, the phone held out to me. "The police want to talk to you."

I take it. The receiver is still warm with her breath. It's Officer Donaldson. He skips the pleasantries. "Eric, we need you to come down and answer some questions."

"Why?" I ask. And in my head, *Again?*

I'd already made my statements, admitted to the pharmacy break-in. I was out on bail for it. The sentence would come later, when the case went to trial. "Does my lawyer need to come too?"

There was a pause on the other end of the phone. "It's not about the break-in."

After I'd made my confession, I'd told the cops about Coach Williams and what he'd done to me. It took hours piecing it all together. Mom had sat beside me, sobbing, clutching her chest like her heart was breaking.

"It's about the other case. We've had someone else come forward."

His voice thuds in my head. "About—about Coach Williams?" I stutter.

"Yes. I can't give you any details, but we'd like to ask you a few questions."

I nod dumbly and hand the phone back to Mom. She'd work out the details. The nightmare that I'd lived wasn't just mine. There was another one, maybe more. The reality made it hard to breathe.

Mom's eyes were wet, the pain on her face as fresh as the night I'd told her everything, sitting outside his house. Shame isn't a weight or something that gets worn. It's elastic, stretching and strangling anything in its reach. But slowly, slowly, the noose was being loosened.

Each day would get better. I had to believe that.

HOPE

The girls were in the common room watching a movie. Huddled together on the couch and in chairs, their shrieks and giggles reached me in my dorm room. Ravenhurst was a different place now that Lizzie was gone. We weren't prisoners to her threats, gossip, and backstabbing. Once she left, the poison she'd spread had disappeared, dissipating like a foul smell.

Emily and Vivian tried to make amends, but it was hard for me to forgive them. They'd been complicit in Lizzie's schemes, standing beside her as she sent texts and emails pretending to be Devon. They'd watched as she sent the photos and done nothing to stop her.

But, they'd told Ms. Harrison and the investigators the truth when they were questioned, confessing their guilt. Lizzie was the only one of them to get expelled. There were no excuses for what she'd done.

Normally, I would have joined the girls in the common room, nestling into the space Cassie had saved for me, but I couldn't tonight. Mom and Eric were coming to pick me up. Dad would arrive later and we'd spend the weekend together at the apartment. Some moments were stilted and full of regret and anger, but at other times, wisps of the family we used to be came back, flitting around us. Giving us hope for what we could be.

A new crop of poems decorated my walls. They weren't hidden against door frames or gouged into the wooden bed frame. I left them out in plain view.

> There are no
> Empty chairs
> At the table.
> We sit,
> All of us,
> Bursting with life.
> Our presence a shout
> For the joy of it.

Through the window, I saw two figures walking across the parking lot towards school. Eric, lanky and stooped compared to the hockey player he once was, and Mom, her frizzy mass of hair poking out from under her toque. As they walked, their boots left a trail in the fresh snow.

Every day, Eric got stronger. A light shone in his eyes that I hadn't seen in a long time. A wave of hopefulness washed over me. We would never be the people we once were. Our lives had been twisted. Diverted. But, we were finding our way back to each other. My fractured family would heal.

ACKNOWLEDGEMENTS

Some authors make writing look effortless—as if novels leap from their fingers to appear fully formed on their computer screens. Sadly, I am not one of them. My stories come out kicking and screaming and have to be beaten into submission. *Finding Hope* began as a very different story, but through many, many (many!) rewrites, ended up being the one that made its way into this book. Thank you to my agent, Harry Endrulat, for his faith in the original *Finding Hope* and for the gentle nudge that sacrificed 40,000 words to make it better. Thank you also to my sister, Nancy Chappell-Pollack, and wonderful friend Cindy Kochanski, for generously giving their time to read and comment on early drafts.

One of the most enjoyable parts of seeing this book come to print has been working with the stellar crew at Dundurn. Thank you to Jennifer Gallinger and Laura Boyle for their artistic talents. A special thanks to Carrie Gleason, Kathryn Lane, and freelance editor Natalie Meditsky for their editorial guidance.

As always, to my husband Sheldon and my boys, James and Thomas, thank you! Writing is a slightly tortuous endeavour, but sharing the journey with them makes it worthwhile.

MORE BOOKS FROM DUNDURN

Under the Dusty Moon
by Suzanne Sutherland

How do you find your voice when your mom is already famous? Vic Mahler is the only daughter of rocker Micky Wayne, whose band Dusty Moon took the world by storm when Micky herself was only a teenager. Now having settled in Toronto, Micky's solo career starts to take off after years spent off the road being a mom. When an offer to tour Japan and Europe falls into Micky's lap, Vic is left to spend the summer in the city without her built-in best friend. Add in a bicycle accident that leaves Vic unable to hold her PlayStation controller, and she may be in for the dullest summer of her life. Fortunately, a sweet stoner boy and a group of feminist video-game makers come along. Can they save the season? And will Vic start to see herself as her own person, away from her mother's shadow?

Merit Birds
Kelley Powell

2015 Dewey Diva Pick

Eighteen-year-old Cam Scott is angry. He's angry about his absent dad, he's angry about being angry, and he's angry that he has had to give up his Ottawa basketball team to follow his mom to her new job in Vientiane, Laos. However, Cam's anger begins to melt under the Southeast Asian sun as he finds friendship with his neighbour, Somchai, and gradually falls in love with Nok, who teaches him about building merit, or karma, by doing good deeds. Tragedy strikes and Cam finds himself falsely accused of a crime. His freedom depends on a person he's never met, a person who knows that the only way to restore his merit is to confess. *The Merit Birds* blends action, suspense, and humour in a far-off land where things seem so different, yet deep down are so much the same.

Throwaway Girl
Kristine Scarrow

Andy Burton knows a thing or two about survival. Since she was removed from her mother's home and placed in foster care when she was nine, she's had to deal with abuse, hunger, and homelessness. But now that she's eighteen, she's about to leave Haywood House, the group home for girls where she's lived for the past four years, and the closest thing to a real home she's ever known. Will Andy be able to carve out a better life for herself and find the happiness she is searching for?

In Search of Sam
Kristin Butcher

Raised by her mother, eighteen-year-old Dani Lancaster only had six weeks to get to know her father, Sam, before he lost his battle with cancer. It was long enough to love him, but not long enough to get to know him — especially since Sam didn't even know himself. Left on the doorstep of an elderly couple when he was just days old, and raised in a series of foster homes, Sam had no idea who his parents were or why they had abandoned him. Dani is determined to find out. With nothing more than an address book, an old letter, and a half-heart pendant to guide her, she sets out on a solo road trip that takes her deep into the foothills, to a long-forgotten town teeming with secrets and hopefully answers.

Since You've Been Gone
Mary Jennifer Payne

Is it possible to outrun your past? Fifteen-year-old Edie Fraser and her mother, Sydney, have been trying to do just that for five years. Now, things have gone from bad to worse. Not only has Edie had to move to another new school — she's in a different country. Sydney promises her that this is their chance at a fresh start, and Edie does her best to adjust to life in London, England, despite being targeted by the school bully. But when Sydney goes out to work the night shift and doesn't come home, Edie is terrified that the past has finally caught up with them. Alone in a strange country, Edie is afraid to call the police for fear that she'll be sent back to her abusive father. Determined to find her mother but with no idea where to start, she must now face the most difficult decision of her life.

Available at your favourite bookseller